SHIFTLESS

SHIFTLESS

A NOVEL

ANTHONY C. MURPHY

atmosphere press

CONTENTS

SHIFTLESS

The employment agency was above a savings bank. It was in one of those old sandstone buildings facing Rochdale Town Hall. Joe said to me, "You go up, I'll wait in the bookies and see what's occurring in the papers!" He touched his finger to the side of his nose so I knew what he meant. He'd had a nap on the horses, a certainty... again... and he wanted to check the form.

"Are you sure, Dad?" I said. "Wouldn't it help if you introduced me to Sandra? Just to make sure they find us something together."

I could see him flinch then. "I can't be talking to her

right now. Sorry. I have other fish to fry... Go on, Seany. It's easy," he said. "She'll see you right. Anyway, you're the one who doesn't want to go to college, the one who said, '*I can't stand anymore education!*'" He mocks me like a kid, because I am one. He doesn't know that I failed to attend any of my exams, so I couldn't go to college even if I wanted to. Then he becomes a dad again. "So, if you want to live with me now, and you're not going to school, you've got to pay... your... rent!" Tapping a tattoo on my chest with his fat finger and laughing as he did so.

"I don't know, Dad. I've only had crappy summer jobs before."

"Well now you can get a crappy all-year-round one!" he said. Then he put his arm around me. "Work is a bunch of bollocks, Sean. We just do it to have beer and fag money. They'll take anyone here. They took me on."

"Yeah, but you didn't have to pass a test," I said.

"Can I help it if some women find me charming?"

"But won't she want to see you anyway?"

"Maybe, but once around the track was enough." He laughs. And with that he scuttled off down the street to the turf accountants.

In the agency I was greeted by Sandra, a red-haired lady candled onto her tiny seat. She had no smile, maybe no lips; it was hard to tell. She looked like a hard lump of wax. I could see why Dad was avoiding her. She had several clipboards on her desk, and I stood in front of her.

"Name?"

"Sean Reilly," I answered, and she looked up at me then. "Hello," I said.

"Age?"

"Eighteen." You had to be at least eighteen to get on at the employment agency, and I was.

"Fill this out, Sean. Take a pew." She twitched her wig in the direction of some more plastic chairs. I took a form and sat down. There were questions on there about where I lived and who with. I hadn't seen Mum in about a year, and I knew she wasn't coming back. I had been living on my own in our old council house. First my mum had kicked my dad out after their last fight, then she had met someone else and moved away. I had the run of the place to myself for a few months, but now my dad had moved back in and taken over. I filled out the forms accordingly. Then I was ushered into another room to do the evaluation.

There was one chair, one table, and one typewriter, and I was handed another clipboard. The papers on this clipboard had the look of a school exam—simple Math and English multiple choice. I took their evaluation tests, remembering to cough and get a few questions wrong. And when it came to the typing test, I did it slowly. I didn't want to wind up in an office after all. Joe had warned me that we wouldn't be working together if I got a desk job. We didn't have a necktie between us.

Following instruction, I brought out my papers, handed them to Sandra, nodded, and then sat opposite her again next to another candidate going through the same rigamarole.

We had our one-on-one soon after. I had passed the evaluation. She seemed pleased for me and lightened up. She even smiled as we went through my options.

I told her I'd rather do nights—more money for all of

us! After all, they made a big commission on their staff. I told her that I was physically fit, but the big question was my own transportation; it was the difference between them giving me a call first or a call at all.

"Well, my dad is on your books and he has a car. We're willing to work together."

"Joe Reilly," she said. "Yes, he phoned our answer service and signed back on with us yesterday." She took a moment in her mind and toyed with a memory. I guess that's what she was doing—that far-away look and the sucking-pen action.

"I hear he's been away." She coughed all perky like.

"He's just got back. Visiting family in Ireland. He thought it would be a good idea for me... if he recommended me."

As Joe had said, it would be the clincher. We would go top of the list. They liked it when a reliable worker on their books had recommended you. Forget nepotism—they needed short cuts. And it solved the problem of me not driving. The agencies couldn't afford to lose clients because of the lack of public transport at nights.

"When can you start?"

I told her I'd start tomorrow, as we were going to get drunk tonight. She was too busy flipping through her job cards and memories to raise one of those eyebrows she used to have.

"We'll start you off with an easy one, warehouse work, see how you go. Be at Seton's in Oldham, Union Street at ten tomorrow night. Ask for Terry."

She handed me two timesheets and some info.

"Your dad can help you with those. Good luck."

I walked down Yorkshire Street a little, toward

Ladbrokes, but he wasn't in there. Maybe he'd already gone on to The Bluebell. I couldn't face a pint yet and it was too cold for window shopping, so I walked over to the ABC to see what was going on.

Dee O'Neill was working the early shift, opening up and cleaning. I banged on the door and she let me in.

"Hey," she said. "Stay out of sight. Heather's in early."

"I left my hat in one of last night's screenings," I joked, as I hadn't seen her in a while.

"Yeah, right!"

I loved the lobby; it was plush red and gold trimmed, like some Victorian music hall from the good old days. I guess the modern clientele was a little incongruous, but they still came. I had worked part time there the year before in the evenings and spent most of my hours tearing tickets then guiding folk in the right direction. I didn't have to talk much; people hardly notice you anyway, just wanting to get a seat before someone else. Everyone wants to get theirs and they don't need an usher. I got the old heave-ho one night after our manager, Heather, found me snoozing at the back of a retro screening of *Flesh Gordon.*

I slinked into screen number three then and that funk of popcorn, coke, and rotting carpet. Dee came in with a brush and shovel and some black sacks. We went down the aisle together; I held her bags for her.

"I got a job."

"Yeah? Doing what?"

"I don't know exactly yet. Seton's Warehouse. You heard of them?"

"In Oldham?"

"Working nights."

7

"The streets will be safe then."

"Yeah, working with my dad."

"Nice! The family business." I think she was being sarcastic. We went through the stalls, tipping the pews looking for lost loot and finding crap. "How's it going? Living with your dad again?"

"It's alright so far. He's been helpful. He seems ... quieter."

"Maybe it's because you're older? You haven't seen him in years."

"Only two and a half," I said. "Not that I was counting."

"Do you want this?" She was holding up a zippo lighter.

"No, I've got one."

"Really? I thought you were going to open up a tobacconist shop?"

"That was just a pipe dream," I said, doing a Groucho impression with a fag butt. She smiled at me, but I could tell she was disgusted.

I found a pound note all rolled up and someone's bus pass. It had the faded photo of a Miss. M. Miggins. I handed the bus pass to Dee to give to the office, and I pocketed the cash.

"I got an interview at a university next week," she said.

"Yeah? Which one?"

"Cardiff."

I suddenly felt dizzy about that distance. I had to sit down. The thought of her leaving was making me sicker than the smell of the fag butt and the carpet.

"What's the matter?" Dee asked.

"Just... everyone is leaving I guess."

"Duh! That's life. You could have too!" she said.

"No, I couldn't, I... I..." My thoughts drifted.

"Your problem is that you never finish anything."

I look at her then and she is busy with her practical life, the detritus of other humans, strangers that she deals with efficiently. It's a flippant thought for her, my lack of seeing things through, and an easy solution that she has found. She's right, I think, she is William of Occam cutting through the bullshit, but for me this is a serious problem. We are so different.

"Listen, I've got to go find my dad," I told her. "Will you be out later on? To celebrate, you know!"

"Maybe."

"Will you be with Dickie?" she asked.

"Nah, he's still not talking to me."

"Well you shouldn't have slept with his girlfriend," she said. She was just trying to wind me up.

"I didn't!"

"I think you protest too much."

"Look it was just a snog," I said.

"Well that's bad enough. Anyway, that's good, because I don't want to see Louise either."

The four of us had always hung around—Dickie and Louise together, me pining for Dee, Dee being nice to me but going out with Derek instead. Derek was okay, but he wasn't one of us four. Anyway, things were changing, had changed already now that she was leaving for good.

"What's up with you and Louise?" I said.

"I told her I might be leaving, and we split up the band."

"No! You were getting gigs," I said. "That's what you wanted... It's what we all want!"

"Well, I can't keep it going from that distance. *If* I get

in... I told her to find a new bass." That distance again. I had to get some air. "Listen, if Derek shows up, I'll see you at six." She smiled at me from behind her bag full of rubbish as I left.

Joe was at the pool table when I walked into The Bluebell. He was playing one handed again to even the odds. I nodded hello to his opponent, one-armed Paddy Brine. "Dad, you should phone that Sandra, back at the agency. She would *love* to see you," but he knew I was taking the piss, as he just grunted in response. I went to the jukebox. Patrick won, so Joe came by and put a fiver in my hand to get a drink. We stayed for a few hours, but Dee never showed. She was probably having a deep talk with Derek. I thought of her more on my way home. Forget her, I thought.

The next night we drove to Oldham by all the old mills, those brick monsters with their glass eyes smashed in. Union Street is in the town centre, but it isn't exactly a twenty-four-hour place. The pubs shut at eleven, so the streets were quiet. Just before our turning was a metal railway bridge. Seton's had it painted with their brand name. I guess the Seton fellas were some big nobs. 'Welcome to Oldham—Home of the Tubigrip Bandage' it said across the riveted girders.

"That's funny," Joe said, pointing it out. "Did you see the new one in Rochdale? 'Birthplace of the Co-op,' only they forgot the hyphen when they first painted it, so everyone thought they invented chicken cages."

"That's funny," I said, but I wasn't laughing.

I was pretty nervous. I always get that way when I go

to a new place, an unfamiliar place, to do others' bidding. I get meek, sometimes mute. It might be different with Joe, but he wasn't laughing either.

The factory was a massive red-brick building that took up one whole block and another for parking. Most of the windows were boarded with big sheets of metal and wire mesh. The name 'Seton' was picked out again with white paint on a tall chimney stack and lit from below in the yard.

Inside, under the white hum of the strip bulbs, we saw that nothing was manufactured here anymore; there was no machinery, only storage and distribution. More than half of the building was vacant now. We walked through vast empty spaces, following signs to the night manager's office. Our boot-steps on the dusty concrete floors echoed off high, pale walls.

Joe was familiar with the routine; he'd been working in these places all his life, on and off, so I didn't have to say much. He clocked us in and went to have a word with Terry. Terry came out to tell us what we would be working at. Terry was only a little older than me, with bright-red hair and a blue uniform with a logo and a sew-on label underneath that read "Home of the Tubigrip Bandage." I got a nudge from Joe, but I had already seen it and I was too busy listening and being reverent. As it turned out there was no need to be—Terry couldn't really be arsed. He sat us down in a corner of the warehouse where there were a few shelves of deflated leather footballs, two hand pumps, and stacks of flat display boxes.

"Stick that in there and go like this and then open these guys up like so and stick that in there." He made a pantomime of it with the balls and the boxes.

"This is the life," Joe said.

And we started to blow up footballs. And then pack them into boxes. And then stack them over there.

We were joined by Ron and Dave, two other agency workers. Ron was an old feller, greasy looking with watery eyes. Dave was a lad. I knew him from school, but he'd turned into one of those swine you see about town wearing a full-on zip-up tracksuit, walking with his arms swinging way out by his sides. One of those lads you have to move out the way of for no reason because it was all for show.

Joe welcomed them both and set about giving them tasks. They must have thought he was the foreman or something because they didn't question. Joe told Dave to start building the boxes and he told Ron to take our newly inflated balls and showcase them just so, in the boxes, and stack them over there.

We had an assembly line.

"Look at this!" Ron said. "This is Great British leather hand stitched in India."

"There and back again. It's a crazy world. At least they've got northern air in them now," Joe said.

"I'm sick of these Paki's stealing our jobs," Dave said as he ambled over for some more cardboard.

Joe rolled his eyes then. "You know these mills used to make all the cotton fabric for the Empire. Gandhi's knickers were probably made right here."

I said Gandhi wore a dhoti, but my dad just called me a smart arse. He and Ron went to the canteen for a fag, which left me with Dave, so I went to get a plastic cup of hot watery tea from the Klix machine. It's the burning of the tongue that keeps the nightshift awake. Dave followed me.

"Didn't you used to go to school at Henshaws?"

"Yes," I said. We didn't ever cross our streams in the showers or anything. I was surprised he remembered me.

"Yeah, I remember Siddiq knocking you out in the hall," he said.

"He didn't knock me out. I slipped. I got up again quite quickly." Jesus, why did I say it like that?

"Ha, I knew it was you. One Punch! You're looking a bit freaky these days."

I think he was referring to my secondhand attire rather than my face.

We resumed our positions after fifteen minutes, except Ron. He hadn't come back. Dave stood over where I was sitting.

"Let us have a go of that. I'm getting paper cuts."

I gave him the hand pump and a bag of spare adaptors. I didn't mind, as my arm was aching. After half an hour Ron still hadn't returned, so Joe went to have a look. I stayed away from Dave in the corner, restacking some of the mess he'd made.

"Oi! Reilly!" Dave threw a ball at me and I managed to trap it with my foot before it hit the wall of shop-ready boxes we'd been building—our pyramid of effort. "Come here a minute."

I booted the ball back at him. He hadn't been on our football team back then, too busy getting off his head probably, so instead of catching, he flinched and it hit him on the shoulder. He was okay about it though. "Nice one," he said.

"What's up?" I said.

"This thing snapped and the new one won't go in."

"That's what the water's for."

He was confused.

"Down there under your chair," I said. "You have to wet it before you slip the little chap in." I was an expert after three hours. He gave a shrug. My dad came back.

"Just seen Terry, Ron's gone home. Apparently he was shitting blood."

"No!" said Dave. "Any excuse."

"It's true. He said he left it in there as proof for Terry."

"That's weird," said Dave and he ran off to take a look.

"You think he's alright?" I asked my dad.

"Yeah."

"He wasn't lying," Dave said when he came back.

"It's a good trick. I'll have to remember that one," Joe said. "Ah, well. More work for us lads, eh?" And he winked at me. Dave groaned, but it was a bonus for us. It meant we wouldn't get finished so we would have at least one more night's work here. After that they might not need us.

We went for dinner or lunch or supper or breakfast, whatever you call that meal you have midway through your working day when it's two in the morning. We had brought a sandwich, and Terry joined us in the canteen with his microwaveable pot. "Curry," Terry said to no one in particular.

It was a brightly lit white room with a few tables and chairs and a kitchen service counter that was shuttered up now. Dave sat with a cup of watery soup from the machine. It was all he had. I nearly felt sorry for him. Joe got up and gave Dave half of his own sandwich.

It was quiet as we ate. Then we heard something drop onto the newspaper on the table, and I saw something scamper on the table in front of us, scurrying away as Dave gave a little whimper.

"It's just a weevil. Probably it was in the lettuce… Crunchy buggers!" Joe said.

"That's the most interesting thing that's happened here in months," said Terry.

We rotated 'duties' and took numerous breaks and swept and restacked and wandered the warehouse, anything to eke out the work. The disadvantage of this was it stretched out the last hours to a snapping point. We were sat pumping our balls again when Dave said, "I don't think I'll be back tomorrow night. It's not worth five quid an hour."

"Whoa, lad!" said Joe. "That's three pints right there. It all adds up. Plus, you can't spend it during the week; you're too busy working and sleeping."

"It might be enough for you, but I wanna look good! And this clobber costs," Dave said pointing at his Nikes.

"Each to their own," said Joe, winking at me. "Some people don't know what to spend their money on. Did I ever tell you about Michael, a feller who worked for me at Rothwell's?"

"No," I said.

"Well, he was a little simple, was Michael. He still lived with his ma when I first met him, only he was thirty-five years old. I don't think he'd been anywhere else in his life. Never left town. Or she wouldn't let him. Anyway, we used to go to The Blood Tub at dinner, and then again after work, only he would never come with us. He'd always go straight home. Said he'd never drank a drop in his life, not even a shandy. He probably gave all his money to the old bat and never had any to spend on himself. She didn't work and he didn't earn that much; he was my part-time general store dogsbody and tea caddy, still he should have had some for himself, don't you think? Then about two years after I met him, his ma died. Michael stayed in the house, the council couldn't throw him out, and he carried on at work, only now he was buying his own food and paying his own bills, with one less mouth to feed and one less body to warm. All the money was his."

"So what did he spend it on?" Dave asked.

"He did what any sane person would do—which makes me think he wasn't that simple after all—he started drinking... Only thing was he didn't know how to go about it. He didn't want to come to the pub, as he was shy of company, so he was a little stuck with it. That's why he came to me. One day he came to my office and he says, 'Joe, you take a drink, what do you recommend I should try if I'd like to get a little tipsy.' 'Well, Michael,' I sez, I tell you what, next time you go to Asda or Tesco or wherever you do your shopping, go down to the booze section and just pick out something that catches your eye. Try it on for size. If you don't like it bring it to me and I'll get rid of it for you.'"

"And did he do it?" asked Dave.

"He must have," I said. "Every Monday, Dad would come home from work with half a bottle of some weird liquor or half a box of wine or something."

"Sometimes," said Joe, "I'd get lucky and he'd bring in a near full bottle of whiskey. He really didn't like the hard stuff. He was really grateful. He was a true altruist."

"I do remember a bottle of Malibu," I said.

"That was all you could handle, Seany. Malibu and milk!" Joe laughed.

"I was twelve!"

Terry came in at six in the morning and told us to go home and see you tomorrow. When we got out of the warehouse the sun had risen but it was cold and we could see our breath and the dust on our boots. Dad drove us home; we were both tired and didn't speak much. I cracked open a beer in the kitchen and listened to Sheila and Vinny waking up through the thin walls between our terraced houses before I headed off to bed.

I woke five hours later with a dry mouth and desperate for a piss. In the kitchen, Joe was frying an egg. He had our neighbour's dog, Lucy, with him. She was slobbering on the floor in anticipation, but she wouldn't be getting any.

"I told Sheila I'd walk Lucy. Are you up for a stroll? This one goes at one mile an hour." He looked down at the bulldog and she flicked her rheumy eyes at him; maybe she thought it was cute. I said I would go. We hadn't walked a dog since Tobyjug died, back when we were all one big happy family. I say happy—there was some laughter bouncing off the walls of the house before Mum kicked Joe out of it and then left it herself for bastards new. It was mainly dry, sarcastic laughter though, nothing to write home about.

It was a fine day, only drizzling a little. We walked up and over Albert Royd's Street then climbed a fence into the field at the end of Howarth Cross's football pitches. Lucy squirmed under, just about. She was a rotund little beast. She was muscle with a muzzle. The grass was long until the banks of the canal where it had been cut back from the slope. We got to the first bridge, a stone arch for a single-lane road linking some farm or other to the main road. Lucy sat down close by the path and wouldn't budge so we all took a breather then. A solitary magpie landed on the bridge and Dad saw it.

"Bad luck! Quick, do you see another one?"

I told him I saw one just fly off, even though I hadn't, otherwise he might fret for the rest of the day. A couple of ducks waited for us to throw some bread, but we hadn't brought any, and anyway it's probably bad for them.

"We used to go catching water hens in Ireland—me and my mate, Maxie. They're pretty slow, easy to trap," Dad said. He was always catching something when he was a kid. Tickling trout or trapping songbirds, like linnets. Where we stood right now, this canal turn, he'd shown me how to catch perch a few years ago. I was about twelve years old, just using a plastic bottle and a piece of string. He cut the bottom out, the dimpled bit, and then put it in the water, the string around the neck. The water would flow in and make it sink, and the fish would swim in, not seeing it, but they couldn't swim out again, because of the hole or the current or both. We caught about five and took them home and put them in an old goldfish tank we still had. They all died within the week and Dad said we should have eaten them before they did. Of course, this was before Mum left. She used to hate it when Dad brought animals home. It was another cause of argument. Anyway, Joe yapped on about his childhood adventures.

"One day, me and Maxie, we did a bunk from school to check our hen trap down by the river. It was about a mile downstream from the town centre. We got near the edge, in among all the reeds and rushes, and there was this big, white... thing... floating... further out but snagged on a low branch. It gave me a peculiar feeling. I already knew what it was, but even though I knew I still had to go through with it and check and see up close with my own eyes. So, Maxie held on to me and I waded in a bit and sure enough it was her."

"Her? Her who?" I asked.

"Well, I forgot to say, but it wasn't important to me. I just knew in the back of my mind what everyone had been talking about on our street. It was this sad lady who had gone missing a few days before. I don't know why she was sad. It's just what all the mothers said, 'Sad auld Mrs. Riordan,' like that. Only she wasn't old. But I knew in the back of my mind it was she before I even got to her. She must have jumped off the bridge in town."

"Why?" I asked, like an idiot.

"I don't know why. She was all white and blue, her face was a real mess, only one eye and she was half naked too. I can still see her. I mean, I stared, for a long time."

"What did you do?"

"We got out of there and headed back in town and telephoned the police from a call box and then we went and hid in the cinema to watch some cartoons."

"Jeez."

"Only thing was the school told the guards we hadn't shown up that day, and they always checked the cinema. So while we were sat there trying to keep our heads down, the lights came on and this officer calls out our full names. Like your Ma when she's angry! We were caught. He marched us home. We were talk of the town though... Sad auld Mrs. Riordan."

"You never found out what it was all about?"

"People didn't talk about stuff like that with their kids. We had to make mad stories up. Then nobody knows what the truth is. She was upset enough to do that, that's all I know."

Lucy rolled over onto her back, showing her white belly.

"I remember walking Tobyjug by the brook," I said. "He loved to go in the water."

"Yeah, he was a holy terrier! Always after water rats."

"They were voles, Dad. Tobyjug and released mink are the reason voles are on the decline."

"Smart arse!"

"Well he'd shake 'em to death before I could get 'em out of his mouth. Anyway, once he was standing in the water, snuffling about, but he was standing on something. It was black and white, I thought it was a cushion that someone had dumped because it was squishy, you know, but when I got to it I realized it was a spaniel. And when I looked up I saw there was a rope swing on the tree. And when I looked down again there was rope around the dead dog's neck."

"That's awful! ... Although. We've all thought of it."

"Killing dogs?" I ask.

"Suicide," he says, staring at the stagnant canal. "It just made me think." Then he brightened a little. "Anyway," he said, "we should do it slowly and enjoy ourselves in the meantime. Eh?"

"Sure," I said. "Animals don't kill theirselves, Dad!" He had me a little worried. "I know who did it to that dog, though. You remember that gang of lads from Foxholes?"

"How would I know what you kids get up to? When was this?"

"I was eleven," I said. "Summer holidays."

"You spent the whole day outdoors. I was working in Manchester in those days."

"Well it was that lot from Foxholes. I had a fight with one of them, fat lad who scratched."

"Did you win?" Dad asked.

"No. I never win." Joe managed to coax Lucy into moving again with promises of a stop off at our local pub, The Entwistle Arms. Joe would be going to meet his mucker, Errol, and Lucy was partial to licking bitter, and maybe a few pork scratchings. I went home for another hour or so in bed.

The phone rang and entered my dream and then my consciousness as it rang again. Joe was still out or sleeping so I had to get it.

It was Dee. Her voice was husky and slow. I guessed she'd had a late one herself.

"Can you come over?"

I didn't need an explanation. I got dressed. Joe's jacket was on a kitchen chair. I took a fiver from his wallet. Maybe I'd tell him later...

I got on the bus to Kirkholt. Dickie's dad was driving.

"Hello, Sean."

"Hello, Mr. Young," I said. "Just to the top shops in Kirkholt please." He rang me a ticket up.

"We haven't seen you around the house," he said as his short-sleeved, hairy arms turned the huge steering wheel and shifted the orange whale of a bus away from the curb and back into the traffic.

"No. Me and Dickie aren't really talking," I said. I just

wanted to sit down now.

"Nothing to do with that Paki girl of his, is it?" he said, looking at the road. "Only, she hasn't been round either. The three of you were thick as my wife's custard two months ago. Anything going on?"

"You'd have to ask him. I haven't... I wouldn't know." I lied. I didn't want anyone else to hate me.

"Aye," he said. "Better get a seat."

"See ya!" I said.

Dee answered the door, but she didn't invite me in. She hustled us away from the house, linked with my arm, then marched us through the gate and down the street.

"What's up?" she said.

"I was glad to get off that bus," I said.

"Dickie's dad was driving?"

"He was. He knows."

"Well. He's probably glad. He never liked Louise."

"Even more so now."

"Well it's not all your fault, or hers. It takes two to fuck, properly, or sometimes, at least two though, I think."

"But we didn't...." Before I could say anything else she just laughed at me.

"Do you need owt from the shop? I need some papers," she said.

"No," I said.

"Oh, dry up! C'mon, let's have a good time, eh?"

She looked all fresh, her short hair still wet from a shower. Her green eyes had a weird look in them. She held my gaze a little too long, so I tried to give her a lustful mental message, but one of her eyes had a slight turn so I don't know if it got through. She walked off into the shop.

She was also a little pigeon-toed. I liked her kinks.

"No," I said again, to the back of her. I didn't need anything. She turned and gave me a grin for no reason though and I was grateful for that.

We made our way to The Lord Howard. It was okay during the day. The sloping sunlight was a screen for the projected tobacco smoke. You could get lost in the swirl for an hour or so. The old doley fellers in there were harmless, only nursing pints of mild while the races were on; we wouldn't get any abuse. Early-doors drinking was lighthearted—the holiday feeling of freedom and moments grasped and savoured. Dee knew the landlord also, or the landlord knew her dad, anyway. Our first pints went down quickly, so we were on our second before she got into it.

"I told Derek about Cardiff."

"He wasn't happy?"

"No. He said it's too far away and we might as well finish now. He says that will give me freedom and peace of mind."

"He's right."

"He is right. It still hurts."

"I guess it would," I said. I knew it would. It was hurting me, and we weren't even together.

"There's no way around it. Even if we say we'll pick up again, we know we won't. We'll have met other people by then. I know he'll want to." I really couldn't bear to think about it. Not only would she not be with Derek but she wouldn't be with me. It was all messed up. What could I do? I could follow her to Cardiff! I could get on a course down there. But I couldn't. I didn't have the A levels and I'd dropped out up here, and now I needed money just to live. I was a dropout full of fantasies that played out as she rambled on. "And if we keep it going, we'll only see each other every six weeks or so and Christmas. It's impractical. We're both sexual people."

"You haven't got in yet; you've got an interview is all," I said, playing it cool again. Jesus, she was driving me crazy. I tried to hold her gaze, but she was thinking too much.

"I know, but I've got a strong portfolio and all the right grades. Plus, it's not everyone's top choice. I chose them first. I'm not a reject from one of the London colleges. They'll see me as a bonus." She winked.

And we raised our glasses and drank to that. And then we had a few more. I was expecting her mum and dad to come in, as we sometimes had a drink together. I think they liked me. They liked me more than Derek anyway. Her mum had told me that one time. It only took one glass of wine for her to tell things like that.

"Are your mum and dad up for a pint?" I didn't know what time it was, as I was feeling a little foggy, so even if I'd looked at the clock it wouldn't have registered.

"No. They're at a Labour rally somewhere," Dee said.

"What about Mikey?"

"They took him with them."

"Oh!" I said. "Of course." He wouldn't be in the house by himself. I liked Mikey. Me and Dee used to babysit him together when her mum and dad were busy with their meetings. He sometimes came to the pub, too, if it was early enough. He was like the little brother I never had, or had somewhere that I hadn't met. I wouldn't put that past Joe. But I didn't see Mikey since Derek had been on the scene. "I thought we could watch *Clue* together or something?"

"Well I'm sure he'll miss you too!" She laughed. "Besides, I've got you to myself tonight." She nudged me. She pushed her knee into my thigh. And I started to get the feeling that something else was going on but I daren't think about that, so I kept it cool. I felt like a confused yet happy idiot.

A song came on the jukebox that she didn't like, or reminded her of something, or someone. We weren't making sense anymore anyway, and the locals had started singing. It was loud and we couldn't talk. She took my hand and led me out of the pub then. I walked her home. She kissed me at her gate, and we went inside. I couldn't believe it, but I didn't question. And then I suddenly felt sad as we walked upstairs. I had this feeling that it would be the last time I would see her. Like she was doing this because we never did and never would do again. But we were here right now and being this close to her body, the warmth of her, us, and her wanting to be with me, me...

I came to thinking I had four legs. I was sweating but cold and I felt heavy. It took me a minute to realize where I was and that Dee was stuck to me, or I was stuck to her. I'd never been here before. She had a single bed and I felt the edge of it in my hip now, a creeping ache spread throughout my body. Then a thought, like a retch, jolted my brain. *What time was it?*

"Hey... Hey! Dee. What time is it? Are you working tonight?"

"Hmm? No. Night off..."

I rolled out of there and found my clothes in the dark. I didn't have a watch, they make my wrist itch, and she didn't have a clock in her room. Who doesn't have a clock in their room? I hadn't a clue what day it was even. It must still be today though. Hopefully.

I got out of her house and made it down to the dark main street. There weren't many people about, but I wasn't stopping to chat anyway. Any glance of any clock or watch face could help soothe my nerves, my itchiness, right now. There were no buses going by neither. It couldn't be that late? How late was it? I walked faster, toward my house. Halfway through the three miles home it started to rain. I cursed everything I could think of, myself mainly, but also my cheap yet stylish boots.

I put my thumb out as I walked...

Another car swashed by. The brake lights seemed hazier each time. Bastards! The thought of them inside their zooming, glowing boxes with a radio, a smoke, some heat, maybe company. I had my balls in my pocket and that was all. I was busy rubbing them together just to keep warm but even they didn't want to know me anymore. They were two little pebbles sucked cold by a tiny ocean of mistakes. Ingrates! And the rain kept coming. It dripped from my head onto my top lip and I tongued the diluted hairspray I had stolen a squiff of in Dee's room. Some of the night was coming back to me. I was disgusted by the taste of myself. I just wanted a cup of tea.

When I got to my front door it was locked. I had a backdoor key so I checked 'round there. My key didn't work. Joe had the deadbolt key and had locked me out. My dad had stuck a note on the bolted door. "Piss Off, Reilly!" I was out for the night. He was at the factory in Oldham by now. Thanks, Joe! I peered over the fence into our next-door neighbour's house. The kitchen was next to ours and their light was on and Vinny was sat there in his vest having a fag. I hopped over the fence and tapped on the window. I saw him jump, startled, and mouth the words, "Jeezus fuck!" I nearly laughed but I was too cold and wet for mirth. He came to the backdoor.

"What's up, lad?"

"I'm locked out."

"Have you tried the windows?"

I said I had but I hadn't.

"Come in then."

Lucy stirred a little on her bed, but she wasn't one for getting up unless she had to. I looked at their kitchen clock and winced.

"Your dad working?"

"Yes," I said. "I was supposed to be."

"Ho, ho! You're in trouble." He had a real look of glee. I knew him and Sheila would be listening at the wall between us later. "All right, lad, take the couch. I'll get you a sheet."

"Thanks," I said. "Any chance of a cuppa?" He scratched the dark bristles on his Fred Flintstone face as if there might be some kind of deal to be struck, but then just nodded.

Lucy was licking my fingers to wake me. I was bursting for a piss, but I stayed prone and kept the sheet on, as Sheila was pottering about getting ready for work and I had a hard-on. Their house was the same as ours but backward like in a mirror and with more plants and floral wallpaper. There was a lot going on in this room. I looked at their council standard gas fire and imagined myself on the other side of the flue watching TV with Joe. I managed to grab my jeans and squeeze my bladder in while Sheila was out of view. I got myself decent before I stood up.

"Morning, Sheila! Mind if I use your loo?"

"Oh! Morning, love! ..." I didn't wait for an answer.

"Listen," she said when I came back out, "would you mind takin' Lucy out for us the rest of the week? I know I asked your dad, but she could do with a bit more exercise and less pork scratchings if you know what I mean."

"Sure," I said.

"Who knows, maybe we'll make it a regular thing. Here take this." She handed me a key wrapped in a fiver. "Let us know how you get on." And she gave my hand a squeeze and jerked her head toward the fireplace. I was about to say, *no take it back!* But I didn't.

I took the dog around the block. I couldn't understand why they didn't just let the dog out to roam, like everyone else did round here. Then again canine life expectancy was low. I waited on the corner until I saw Sheila leave, then I put Lucy back in their kitchen, locked the door, and shuffled off back home.

He heard me in the kitchen. I was putting the kettle on when he pounded downstairs. He was in his ratty dressing gown. His face was crumpled and red and he looked older. I turned away from him and opened a cabinet door to take something or other out. He must have leapt forward then, as there was a loud smack and the open door cracked into my face and bounced back. It forced me to crouch down in a daze for a second and hold my head to keep it from falling off. He stood over me and pointed his finger with one hand and closed the cabinet door with the other. I looked at him then, his eyes were fronting his glasses, glittery and mean. I could see the green and sleep in them; they didn't shy from mine, or shake, as they sometimes did.

"I don't care where you were," he said. "I'm not your mother. Don't treat me like it. You can't pull the shit you pulled on her with me." He stabbed himself in the chest with a finger "Boozing with your mates when you should be working. Taking advantage. Taking the piss!" I didn't say anything about how he'd treated Mum. I had no smart-arse comment. He was liable to smack me again and I was still dizzy. "Oh, and that job's finished. Take those in." He pointed to two timesheets sitting on the kitchen table, then went back up to bed, muttering.

I had called Dee and we arranged to meet in town. I had to see her. She couldn't feel half as fatalistic as I did about last night because she agreed immediately. I was waiting in Our Price flicking through vinyl. She came up behind me and made some comment on my perusal choice. "The Pogues are a bunch of shite!" What did she know? She liked Japan.

"Hello," I said, but she wouldn't look me in the eye for very long. We both felt awkward. We didn't kiss. She noticed the swelling on my cheek, but she didn't ask. I sighed a little, but she didn't pick up on it either. We spent a while in there, as they were playing some decent music.

I bought a Woodentops cassette for two quid fifty. That left me enough for two pints. It was still early though. I felt the timesheets in my jacket pocket and thought how all that pretense of me being a working man didn't really matter now that she was leaving.

"I have to go down the street a bit. Come on."

"Where to?"

"Just an agency."

"I knew you didn't have a job."

"I did have one." I hadn't told her it was temporary. "Come on. Buy you a pint after."

"I'm hungry," she said.

We wandered down the hill toward the agency office and I nipped upstairs to see Sandra. She took the timesheets off me and read them over. 'That's two nights for the two of you." I nearly corrected her mistake, but I didn't. "Sorry you had to do all the work. But you really saved us. We're grateful you got the job done. We had words with those other two."

"Dave?"

"And Ron, yes. I know it's tedious work but it's decent rates at Seton's... good rates at Seton's. It's a shame they're winding down. We got a lot of work from them."

"Yeah," I said. "Nice place." No wonder Joe was so mad at me—Joe had done the work of four. I owed him.

"I have something for you two in Littleborough. Starts tomorrow night. Can you make it?"

"Sure!" I said. "We'll be there."

"Here," she said, handing me the info. "You ask for Gary."

I bounded down the steps in the mood to celebrate again, but when I got outside I saw that Dee was in an argument with a skinhead. My adrenaline level couldn't take this. I hung back a little. I recognized him from The Fusiliers, the pub where we would get our speed from. All kinds went in that place and this feller was all kinds mixed into one. His name was Tony, and he stood six foot five-ish in his boots and braces, and he was a fully fledged member of the National Front, down to the Nazi tattoos. I'd seen him jump on three of the local Bangladeshi lads at the town festival, and he hadn't fallen. They had to back off in the end; a couple of them looked broken. It was sickening but what could I do? He was an animal. If there was one thing that scared me more than police dogs, it was skinheads. He was accusing Dee of being one of 'that bunch,' the Anti-Fascist League, and distributing leaflets that were unpatriotic. She was busy denying it and defending it at the same time. He was getting angry so I stepped in.

"What's up?" I asked.

"Oh, another one," said Dave and he grabbed what was left of my worn-out jacket lapels and pulled me up to his height. He lifted me off my feet.

"Listen, I think you've got the wrong people. We don't do anything," I said.

"Well it looked like you. You all look the same to me, punks!" He spat. I thought that was a bit much; he was the one wearing a uniform and a skin helmet.

"He's right," said Dee, "but if we did do anything it would be the *opposite of you.*"

"I don't think she means that," I said. "She's just a little...you just caught her by surprise." I had air beneath my feet and was thankful when we all heard some random voice shout, *"Nice one, Cyril!"* so we all turned to look. We knew what it meant, some stupid song in the charts, but it was used to herald the most famous man in Rochdale, wherever he went. "Nice one, Cyril! Nice one, son. Nice one, Cyril, let's have another one!" Sure enough, Cyril Smith, our big Member of Parliament was out shopping, in fact he'd just come out of Dixon's. He was carrying a plastic bag and wearing his slippers. He shuffled off toward the stationers, shaking hands occasionally. He always reminded me of Alfred Hitchcock, appearing here and there for no reason. Tony let me down and spat, "Another one. He lets them all in," pointing at Cyril. I pictured Tony trying to lift up that twenty-nine stones of professional argument as he shoved me against a doorway. "That's why there's no work for us," he said with a long finger poking my clavicle, before he turned to watch Cyril's wobble. I could see Dee was about to say something forthright about the Fourth Reich, but I saw an open window in his distraction. I grabbed Dee and we slipped off in the wake of Cyril's interference, disappearing into the crowd of shoppers.

"I hate them all," Dee said.

"Forget it. Come on! Let's celebrate. I got another job!"

We were at the bar in The Bluebell having a heated debate about The Top of The Pops.

"At least they'll have The Jesus and Mary Chain on."

"But it's still got wankers like Jimmy Saville presenting!" Dee protested.

Joe came in, put some money in the jukebox and "Elusive Butterfly" came fluttering over the airwaves. Joe winked at Dee as he walked past toward the pool table where Patrick was setting them up. Those two blessed each other in greeting and began to play.

"I hate Val Doonican," I said.

"Oh! You can hate someone as inoffensive as Val Doonican, but you can agree with a Nazi?"

"Huh?"

"You know, you should grow up a bit, Sean. Why don't you go back to college?"

"Like Derek?"

"Yes, like Derek. Like me, too. You'll end up being stuck here."

"Well, I can't stick college. Bunch of pretentious arseholes," I said.

"You're sad, Sean. Open your eyes. There's a bigger picture than just you... I can't wait to leave this place," she said, and got up. "I'm going."

"You didn't have to wait long," I joked.

"You know what I mean!"

"Yeah. Well. See ya then."

"'Bye!" She squeezed my hand, the same as Sheila had done earlier. It reminded me of the five-pound note actually. I was thinking of that and not Dee as she left. I couldn't tell her that I was just crap at college. I didn't get it. It was impossible for me to learn and I felt stupid. I couldn't tell her that because I wanted her to think of me as something good. But here I was thinking about money. I needed money to get another pint. There was nothing to be done between us. She'd left half her drink, so I combined it with mine and went up to speak to the old feller.

"Hey, Pop!" I said

"What's up?"

"Thanks for covering for me last night."

"No one else showed." He shrugged. "Terry left me to my ownsome. I just made like you were there busy doing something." He wasn't angry with me anymore. He'd had some sleep.

"Here!" I handed him his pay and an extra fiver. "We've got a job tomorrow night in Littleborough." I dug out the info from my back pocket.

"Hurry up, Joe! You're spots," Pat said. Joe took his shot, missed, and came back to me.

"Beswick's Sauce Factory," he said. "Should be more interesting than blowing up balls."

"I guess."

"Nice-looking lass you're with."

"Oh. I'm not with her."

He handed me back the fiver. "Go get us a drink. Pat just wants half." Patrick grumbled something behind him. Joe touched my bruised cheek and said, "Sorry about that," he said, "but you can't con a con man." He always knew when I sneaked cash off him.

We left early the next night so Joe could give me a driving lesson. Cars were new to all of us. Mum didn't drive and Joe had only just got enough together to buy his own vehicle. I didn't even know what make it was. There was a supermarket car park that was empty by eight, except for the stoners and the occasional boy racers meeting up or taking a breather. It was a clear night, cold and bright. I choked the engine then hopped about a bit in first. I managed to get to second gear, then tootled around the tarmac and got into the swing of the thing. I could hear laughter outside from other kids, but Joe was pretty patient. He waited until I could drive in perfect circles before he took over again.

Joe drove us up the Halifax Road. We used to drive up there years before, with my mum's dad, Grandad to me, when we went to Hollingworth Lake. Grandad was the only one with a car in those days. It was a Maxi, with leather seats, and he smoked cigars, which made me sick, so there was always a bucket in the back for me to throw up into, for the longer journeys anyway. The lake was like our seaside, living fifty miles or more from the nearest beach. We were always there on bank holidays, along with half the town. There were tales that there was a monster pike in the lake that no one could catch. I remember how disappointed I was to find out that the lake was man made, a reservoir overspill, and that the fish wasn't even a myth, just a joke.

"Have you heard from your mum?" Joe asked.

"She sent me a letter with some money a while back."

"How much?"

"Just a tenner," I said. She'd been gone a year now, and that was all I'd heard.

"Well I guess it gets expensive down in London. Still, I thought this new guy was loaded."

"I guess. Compared to us."

"You know. I'm sorry for that, Seany. It was my fault she was left on her own with you, but you could have helped her, behaved yourself."

"It was your fault she threw you out," I said.

He laughed at that. "You weren't there. You don't know what happened." That was true. One day the family was just no more. It was like waking up in a different dream. Neither of them had told me what had happened, but she had a black eye for a while afterward.

"Well, I could guess," I said. My own cheek was bruising up nicely.

"That's only half of it," he said.

"What's the rest?" I said.

"She'll have to tell you that," he said. "You know she would have taken you with her, if you were younger. Or a girl."

I looked at the stars over the reservoir and wondered whether there had ever been a time when we were all happy together. There must have been one. Maybe I had been too young.

"Why did you come back though?" I asked him.

"She asked me to. To look after you."

"I was doing alright on my own," I said.

"No you weren't. No work, signing on, and you stopped going to school. You had your chance to make a go of it... You know, Vinny and Sheila were keeping an eye on you? They told your mum what was going on and she phoned me, told me you were up to all sorts of shenanigans. Loads of people around all the time. Up all hours."

"Well I had to get a roommate. The council wouldn't let it be sole occupancy."

"Anyway, I thought it was about time I did something... right? Plus I only had a little flat where the council put me in Burnley."

"So, you came back for you then?" I said.

"Yeah." He sucked that word in when he said it.

We drove on to Whitelees Road, where the sauce factory

was. It was a modern building, purpose built. Once inside we saw the machinery was all new, stainless and smooth with only an occasional hydraulic hiss bursting the low hum of the mechanics. There was an overwhelming smell like hot sugar and vinegar, which bit into your nostrils. A couple of workers were busy in the stockroom. They wore white overalls, blue surgical gloves, hairnets, and hardhats. It was all a bit different from Seton's. We made our way to the night manager's office up a scaffold-like staircase into an elevated portakabin that looked down on the whole factory floor.

Gary sat at a desk. He had a hairnet on but no hard hat. He had piercing blue, smiling eyes and a fat ginger moustache on a skinny red face.

"Welcome! Have a seat!" He looked at us both. "Are you brothers?" he asked.

"Something like that," my dad said.

"Uh-huh," said Gary. He wasn't arsed, he was writing something.

"So, we've got two staff on holiday, two positions to fill for two weeks: one for a packer and one for a stacker. It's not difficult. Our supervisor, Dean, will take you through it. Do either of you drive a forklift?"

"I do," said Joe, showing Gary his license.

"You'll be the stacker then, Joe. I'll get you some clobber, lads. Follow me!"

The supervisor, Dean, was a rugby player by the cut of him. His hairnet and white overalls made him look like a big brother at a kid sister's dress-up birthday party. He made me wear something similar that engulfed me and then showed me around and walked me through the first steps of sauce industry; 'this goes here and that goes there again and whatnot.'

I took my place with three other workers at the arse end of a machine that shat out little plastic tubs filled with hot ketchup. I didn't mind wearing this gear; it made me feel anonymous, less self-conscious, in context of course. I was a part of the engine now... Although it was the first time I'd worn all white in my life... The tubs came out fast in sixes on a conveyor belt. I had to pick them up and pack them in a box in layers of twenty-four in four layers. It's not hard to pick up six little tubs with two hands, but to swing back and forth and get them packed neatly so that they all fit meant that I rushed and spilled and dropped a fair few in the first hour. The other three seemed to use minimal movements, hardly shifting their feet at all. Luckily the machine didn't run continuously. It was overfilling or missing the tubs, or the machine operator hadn't loaded properly, so there were chances to catch up.

At the end of an hour the full boxes were sealed and put on a pallet. Joe drove over on his forklift truck and picked up the pallets, took them to the dock, wrapped them with a shrink-wrap machine and loaded them onto a wagon. When the whole thing got a rhythm going you didn't notice the time, and before I knew it there was a bell ringing for a break. The machines came to a stop, and everyone made their way to the staff room. I was sweating.

Gary was in there, at the microwave with some leftovers. Joe came in and brought our sandwiches. There were lots of tables, but we all sat close.

There were only ten on the nightshift, just enough to

keep the place ticking over and fulfill some orders. During the day, Gary told us, there could be fifty working on the machines and another twenty making the sauces. It was a young operation and they only had four contracts so far, but they were national ones.

"So," said Joe to Gary, "how did you get this job?"

Before he could answer, Dean, through a mouthful of food, said to Gary, "It's okay, we can ignore him, he's Irish." Gary laughed. I blushed. I couldn't look at Joe. He got it in the neck sometimes. I was able to hide behind my accent and my birth certificate, Mum being English. I pretended I was busy eating. Dean laughed and he and Gary started talking about something else. Joe left his sandwich and got up and went out. I sat finishing my food trying to be invisible, then got a coffee and quietly left the room. I found Joe outside smoking a cigarette.

"Good job, this," he said. "I bet they pay well if you can get on the books. You should apply."

"What about you?"

"Sean. No one gives a fuck about me. And no one gives a fuck about you. Not really. Everyone tries to get what they want or tries to get away with what they can get away with. We're all a bunch of fuckers and we're all fucked... These aren't my kind of fuckers."

"What kind?" I asked.

"Some of these English fuckers," he said.

"I'm an English fucker," I said.

He laughed. "That you are, son! Anyway, Errol might have something lined up at his place." Something tickled him then, his dark look dropped, and he gave a little chuckle. "Errol got arrested last week."

"Is that funny?" I asked.

"Well, he was driving in town and got pulled over for a red light, only he didn't have his license on him."

"They arrested him for that?"

"No. He kept telling them his name was Errol Flynn and they thought he was taking the piss. They hauled him into the station. Of course he couldn't prove it."

"That's not funny."

"Well, he was laughing when he told me."

The next batch they made was barbecue sauce. I didn't care much for that, but at least we had a little variety. During a machine breakdown, Dean asked me to help at one of the mixers. The feller in charge of the mixer needed ingredients. He gave me a printed list. He needed sugar and fructose. A one-tonne bag of white sugar was hooked to the roof beam and you released a spout at the bottom once you had a wheelbarrow in place—a clean, stain free, steel wheelbarrow. The sugar poured out and threw up the sweetest dust storm that ever choked you. I rolled the full barrow over to the guy and went to get the other stuff. The fructose was stored in massive vats and poured through a tap until you had a tank full of clear, sticky liquid. I imagined swimming in it. This place was swimming in it. There was some kind of sugar in everything they made. We were drowning in it.

I was back at my post when the shift bell went. My back was aching from constant twisting and I was happy to see the morning through the high narrow windows. I met Joe out at the car.

"Well?" he asked.

"It went quickly, don't you think?"

"Shall we come back then?"

"I guess so." I thought there was enough going on in there to keep from getting bored.

I walked Lucy around the block when I got back, then I went to bed for six hours. When I woke it was time to walk her again, so I took her over the field along the canal. It was a routine that I would follow for the next two weeks. It was good to get out and I was starting to enjoy the walks more than the dog.

I kept to myself, and only saw Joe when it was time to come and go to and from the factory, as we worked in separate sections now. We fulfilled our time there. No one wanted to talk to us, not unless they were giving orders. They saw us as temporary, not real workers with contracts. Not a part of the union. We wouldn't be around for very long. We ate at separate tables. My dad's idea was that I may get a real job out of it. He only spoke to one other feller, the guy who drove the wagon in and out. He got his orders and kept his head down. I had to deal with Dean, but I hardly spoke to him. We all tolerated each other. I got driving lessons and learned how to make blue cheese dressing and stopped dropping boxes and that was that. At the end of our last shift we got our timesheets signed and walked out of there to no farewells. I thought Joe was going to slash Dean's tires or something; his mind must have been elsewhere. I felt strange about the place; the attitude in there was sour and insular and I didn't want to belong to that, so I didn't apply for a full-time job, but I told Joe I had.

I walked into town on the Saturday morning before going to bed. I knew the agency closed at lunch, so I wanted to catch them open and make sure we got paid before the next week. I walked down the backstreets, off the main road, as it was quicker. Up ahead I saw what I knew to be two young lads giving another lad a kicking. Even at a distance you just know it. My legs carried me over there to go and stop it. I didn't even think. The lad on the ground wasn't making any noise and the two rearing over him only shouted occasionally. I walked calmly toward them. As I got nearer, I saw they were all my age or younger. The two doing the kicking were Pakistani lads, or Bangladeshi. I didn't ask. They looked about fifteen years old.

"Hey. Come on. He's probably had enough."

They stopped and looked at me then.

"He's a fuckin' junkie," the taller one said.

"Okay," I said. "But you got him."

"This is our street. He's in our doorway."

I looked down at the figure slumped against the wall. It was Dave, the lad, from Seton's. He had no swagger about him now. He looked a mess, all swollen up like a football, but he wasn't bleeding. They were right—this was their area nowadays, their backdoor. Still, it was a quiet street away from anyone he knew, and he'd just ended up there by chance.

I looked back up at them. The smaller one of the two shifted on his feet and smirked and looked away. The other one, though, the one who was talking, his brown eyes glittered. He stared right into me. He was breathing heavily, like he couldn't get a handle on it; I thought that he wanted to hit me, too. He probably did. He probably wanted to hit every white man he met. I couldn't help that. Or maybe I could.

"Come on," I said, "I'll give you a free shot." I pointed to my chin. "A free punch and then we'll get out of your street." The little one snickered again and came right up and punched me, shouting, "We don't need your permission!" He didn't really connect but I made out like he did.

"Hey!" I said. "Come on! Oww, that hurt!" and other such nonsense.

"Fuck off! FUCK off!" The big one was giving an order. Like it was his idea. I helped Dave up and we moved on slowly but not before they spat on him. They stood their ground and watched as we rounded the next corner.

"Ta, mate!" Dave said.

"Are you okay?"

"I am flying." He didn't recognize me.

"Here, let's just get across the road," I said. I was trying to get him to the bus station, to a public place where I could leave him. The only trouble was we had to get over John Street and we were stuck in the middle, so I had to listen to him. He was out of it and I did think about the infirmary for a second, but he was high still, he'd be in trouble.

"You ever tried glue? You should. It makes you fly."

He didn't care. Maybe he couldn't feel the bumps. I think he'd forgotten already.

"Do you know worms play rugby?"

"You'll be okay," I told him. "You're okay." I said it in a soothing voice. I didn't know much about it, but I didn't want him freaking out and thinking I was a giant Mars bar or something. That's the only thing I'd heard about it. It was always Mars bars. I got him to a bench in the bus station and sat down with him. He kind of drifted off a bit and I distanced myself and waited until everyone who had seen us arrive together had gotten on their buses...then I sidled off through the depot. It was getting busy. The town centre on a Saturday. I merged with the stream of people heading for the shops.

Sandra gave me a warm welcome. She was getting friendlier by the job. The agency was pleased with our performance, or more likely our punctuality and attendance. They had another job lined up for us already. This one was in Castleton at Woolworth's warehouse. It was a big place. Anyone could get a job there, and it was a fast turnover. It was full of skites, my dad said. I knew a few who had done at least a day's work for them and everyone hated it. Sandra said it was all they had on nights at the moment, unless I wanted to do days at Manchester Health Authority performing data entry. No I didn't. I couldn't be sitting at a desk all day. We could handle Woolworth's. I walked back home as it started to rain. I had cash in my pocket and another week's work sorted for Monday. It was time to celebrate again after breakfast.

Inside the white terrace front of The Entwistle Arms, I sat at the bar finishing a pint of Thwaites' Original. The place was carpeted and wallpapered just like anybody's front room—knickknacks and keepsakes and brass pots, family portraits everywhere. I asked Big Dave, the barman, for another pint of distraction from the ordinariness. He was sat on one arse cheek on his high wooden chair going over the form in the racing paper. Joe and Errol were playing darts in the side room. We were the only customers, apart from Lucy, the bulldog, at my feet.

What a day.

The day, this capsule, had a numb beauty to it distilled by the quietude of nowhere and no one to be. It made me sigh. Aaah! I was full of love for mankind, my neighbour, my distant quiet neighbour, mankind. I would have swooned right there but I didn't want to miss a moment. There was a fire inside and a torrent outside. There was peace and there was comfort and there was nourishment here. There was a cyclone of turmoil elsewhere. I drank down another draught.

Oh my lord I love the day off.

"Do you want a game, lad?" Errol punctured my reverie with a dart. No, I couldn't handle any competitiveness. They joined me instead.

"A pint of diesel!" Joe ordered as Dave picked his brains over the Newmarket meeting.

"I hear you got arrested," I said to Errol. He was older than Joe, a big man with a big grey moustache and a big nose to go with it. Or vice versa.

"Oh that. 'Tweren't nowt," he said as he nibbled on a pack of PK. "All cleared up. It happens now and then. It's like that song, 'A Boy Named Sue.'"

"You could change your name."

"Who does that but rich folk? Anyway it's a bit late now."

"You don't know what his middle name is."

"Stop that, Joe," Errol said.

"Why? What is it?" I asked. But no one answered.

Two women walked in then, under the cover of one umbrella. They shook themselves by the doormat, primped their perms, and took off their coats. They had uniforms on, half-day Saturday staff from a factory down Buckley Road on their way home, probably. One of them was as tall as Errol.

"Two halves of lager, Dave!" Joe ordered again.

"Hello, Joe!" the tall one said. Her friend lurked behind.

"What do you know, Sharon?"

"I know it's nice weather for ducks," she said.

"And fish!" Joe said, raising his glass.

"And the thirsty!" Errol said, raising his.

"The rabid," I said.

"The rabbits!" Joe and Errol said in unison and drank.

"Sharon, meet my son, Sean. Sharon works up at the prison there."

"Oh yeah! I used to deliver your newspapers," I said. I didn't know what to say. Buckley Hall was on my route when I was a kid. The place used to terrify me on dark mornings.

"Well...," she said, "thank you! ... Cheers for the drink, Joe!" She and her friend took themselves to a snug and sat down.

"You charmer!" Errol pinched my cheek.

"That Sharon, she's long enough to be continued," my dad said.

"And the other one had a face like a rivet catcher's glove," Errol said.

They rudely laughed at each other's banter and turned their attention back to the bar then and the important business of fifty-pence accumulators.

At ten to three in the afternoon, last orders rang, so we ordered one more. The place had filled a little, but we had our bubble at the bar that the bit part players had entered for a brief how-do-ya-do moment before drifting backstage, and now we were the last left again. Dave had gone for a nap, so his wife, Anne had to kick us out—and after my dad had been whispering in her ear.

The three of us went to our house. I nearly forgot I had Lucy with me. I walked her around the block and let her water the corner before I took her back home. Vinny was in. He gave me another fiver for the week as I swayed and dripped on his porch mat. I hadn't noticed it was still raining.

Joe and Errol were snoozing in armchairs. The gas fire was on three bars and the TV was showing the horses. I contemplated switching over to the channel with the viddy printer to see the football scores coming in, but I guessed I could use some sleep too, so I went to bed. I wondered what Dee was up to. I pictured her face and thought I could smell her and drifted off into some twitchy dream of her touches.

After an hour I got up. The results were coming in and my dad was checking his pools. Errol had been home and come back again with some of his own-made rhubarb wine. I made myself some toast and watched for the scores. It was a dire day for them. No one won, no one I liked. I thought that was the way. When your life is going okay someone has to suffer and it was usually your team. Or maybe I wasn't wearing my lucky socks. Joe screwed up his coupon and threw it at the telly.

"I don't know why you bother," Errol said.

"You never know," said Joe.

"While you're busy waiting…," Errol said as he poured out some wine.

"I have something else." Joe got up and went to the cabinet. "It's about the only thing the family gave me. That and a couple of the old feller's medals." He brought out a clear bottle of clear liquid. "A drop of poison?" He shook the bottle for effect.

"What is it, Joe?" Errol said. "Is it poteen?"

"Yeah!" said Joe.

"What medals?" I asked. Joe got three small glasses, gave us all a pour.

"Taste this, sonshine! It'll put hairs on your hairs…Well, how is it?"

"Good. Taste like oranges," I said. "With a kick."

"Well they make it out of anything over there. Potato skins, eggshells, used teabags…I got it from a scoundrel in Rafferty's, Clonakilty."

"What?" I nearly spat. It sounded like the fuel for the DeLorean in *Back to the Future*.

"Don't worry. The alcohol kills all the germs." Joe laughed.

"What medals?" I asked again.

"Yeah. I'll go get them."

He came back with a box and started to go through it.

"Look at this." My dad handed me an old photograph. It was brown and white and some of the image was worn away, but still you could see it was a group of soldiers in two rows. The front row was seated and included a couple of white men in the centre. The back row, standing, were all Indian. I knew from school that a part of the Raj had been conscripted to aid the First World War effort. They wore turbans and puttees and British army boots.

"That's your grandad there. He was an army cook." He pointed to the white feller on the left front. "Those must've been his kitchen wallahs," Joe said.

My dad had brought this stuff back after they had finally sold the Auld House in Cork. That place was full of dreams. The Auld House of Joe's past, where he grew up in the '50s with his brother, Don. The memories they had. And also the dreams of what we could do with the money when it sold. My mum had clung on to those dreams. But Granddad had died years ago and Uncle Don had clung on to the brick and mortar, and the Auld House never sold. Not for years.

"Where was this photo taken?" I asked, turning the picture over in my hands. It even smelled old.

"I don't know. France, Belgium? He never talked about it."

"Never?"

"Not to me. My da was mealy mouthed anyway but he was loath to talk about those days. There was a split back then, you know? Some Irish in the British Army were seen as traitors," Joe said. He handed me two medals, not for valour as far as I could tell, but service medals, with *Pvt. Sean Reilly* inscribed on the rim. Me and my granddad had the same name. "I think secretly he was proud to do some kind of duty, but he would never say. You see, while he was away the rebels had got more support for their cause, so when he came back it was all different. His brother and some of his friends had taken to the hills with others and were fighting a guerilla war against the British army. They won... eventually, but... Some families still don't talk about it."

"You never saw these before?" I asked about the medals.

"I never saw any of it until we cleared out the house. I bet those guys," he points at the Indians, "went back to fight against the Brits too. And good luck to them."

We all took a drink.

"Me and Don went through the house. There wasn't that much stuff for a long life. You remember that house? It had been vacant for years. No buyers. We sold it for nothing, or next to nothing. Well, it was nothing."

I had been to Ireland a few times, staying with cousins, but I'd only been to the Auld House once when I was six years old. All I remembered about the place really was that it had no water upstairs and we had to go outside to a shed for the toilet. I remembered my grandad's face though, long and droopy as it was with blood-red eyes underneath where the skin was fallen, and I remembered his mouth was in constant motion, not talking but slurping and maybe clacking in disappointment.

"He made us banana butties," I offered. "Did you stay there?"

"I had to. Me and your Aunt Maureen don't exactly see eye to eye, so Uncle Don thought it was best... That house," he sighed. "Banana butties! It was about all he would eat; he had no teeth... Did you know he was the town baker when I was a lad? Hardly ever saw him... always up early... He was strict. Took the pledge when he came back from the war apparently, never had another drink. He ran the local scout troop, too. That's what I mean about the army. I think he was proud of his duty. And then when I was older I used to see him standing on that bridge looking out, watching the river flowing away from the town. He never left again though. He never went anywhere."

I passed the photo back. Errol had been sitting there quietly watching us.

"When did you come over, Joe?" he asked.

"1967."

"Did you see him much?" Errol asked.

"Once or twice," Joe said.

It got to half past six and we left the house to get some tea. There was a queue in the chippy. It didn't matter. It was warm. Up on the tiled wall behind the range was a huge poster with every kind of food fish that gets caught in the North Sea. They only served you cod and haddock here, though, maybe a crab cake.

I had been studying the picture for years; it was yellow and faded now. There were fish that looked so strange and different that it made me wonder whether I would get to be anywhere else than here. Was someone in the world having coelacanth and chips for tea? Deep fried as a matter. I reveled in the aroma of chip fat. The memories of Mum when she would come home late from work to tuck me in, her hair full of the smell. I must have been ten when she had that job. I found that comforting, but Joe was the opposite. He would admonish her for it, yelling at her to wash. And on his bad days he'd do worse.

The food was worth the wait. I felt like I hadn't eaten in days. I needed stodge. Chips and gravy, rice and mushrooms. The others got the cod out of habit, but it wasn't good on the weekend. You had to get it mid-week, I told them. I knew because I had worked there for a month, when I was fifteen, just on Saturday lunchtimes serving at the counter. That was before the new tenants had taken over and had a whole family full of their own help.

The chippy was next door to The High Sheriff, so we went in there for one when we'd done. The High Sheriff was quite big compared to The Entwistle. It had a pool table and a jukebox and was generally busier. I didn't like it much, as I had played against their Sunday league side and my memories were like bruises, immediate to the touch.

"Hello, Joe!" said the young barman. "Who's the freak?"

"Hello, Bob, this is Sean. You know Sean!"

"So it is, didn't see him for the hairdo. Hello, Sean!"

"Ah!" my dad said when I didn't reply.

Bob was only messing; we'd known each other for years. He didn't care much for me now, though, being one of Dickie's mates from before me. He had to have a little dig. Maybe after that I would be ignored. I didn't care much for him either. We ordered three whiskeys and found a table.

"You know Nico drank in here?" I said.

"Who's that?"

"She was a singer in the late sixties. She was supposed to have lived round here somewhere."

"I never saw her," Errol said. Not that he knew who she was. Maybe he did.

We didn't stay long. The music was too loud so we drank up.

"Come on," Joe said. "I don't like Simple Minds."

"Nor do I," I said.

Back in The Entwistle, Anne lined up three delicious pints. The beer went down faster than Tobyjug at a rat hole. I remember seeing Dad whispering to Anne again whenever Big Dave was out of sight, and I remember giving Errol an easy win at a game of darts. I remember. The night slipped into an easy oblivion, a light-hearted, goofy-faced grin of an evening, a worthwhile celebration of the week, a drunken punctuation.

Monday and bloody Woolworth's warehouse. Like Seton's, it was a onetime mill. It was a massive box-shaped red-brick structure with an out-of-commission smokestack. This one had all its windows though and new heavy-duty security doors, and a guard to go with them, and a gate and a tall, spiked metal fence to go with the gate. They had done their anti-vandal classes. There was no graffiti and you couldn't even piss on the wall on the way home from the pub if you were of that mind and bladder. You just wouldn't reach.

A few of us started the same night. We were all from agencies. Woolworth didn't hand out night-shift contracts when it could get staff with no rights to paid breaks or holidays. We were handed temporary passes and ushered in by the security guard.

The interior of the warehouse was freshly painted and peppered with notices, most of them warnings or health and safety regulations. There was a sign on the stairwell above our heads while we were walking up to the Induction Office, "Beware on the Stair." A threat.

We went through an introduction and were then told to report to Loading Manager, Darryl.

The radio was blaring down on the dock. It was Radio 1, but that wasn't too bad at night. The dock was a raised concrete bay that could fit ten wagons backed up—big articulated wagons with two decks worth of stacking.

Darryl wore a blue lightweight raincoat and carried a clipboard full of worksheets. He looked younger than Joe, and he looked stressed. We were split into four teams of four and out of each team one person was designated team leader—Joe was ours, as seniority rules. Joe was given a tick sheet full of order numbers and little stickers. It was very technical—Darryl explained loudly.

Each order number corresponded to an item somewhere on the shelves. You had to go and 'pick' it from the shelf, put the sticker on it, pack it in your crate and go get the next item and so on until your crate was full. Full crates were stored on the dock until an empty wagon was available, then they were loaded on and sent around the North West to individual retail outlets.

The warehouse was vast, and items were randomly ordered by numerous shops and could be at either end of the place; because of this we were given electric trucks that held up to three crates so we could tootle about the stores. The little trucks had a maximum velocity of 14 m.p.h. They also had a tight turning circle and a dead man's brake.

"Oh!" said Darryl. "There's a quota to fulfill. If you don't fulfill it, we won't be needing you back tomorrow night."

"What is it, this quota?" someone asked.

"It's so many items per hour."

"How many?"

"So many." It was clear Darryl didn't care much. He was probably the reason for the fast turnover of workers.

The place had everything from electrical goods to clothing to penny chews. I was busy for an hour getting to grips with the truck and the shelving system and the layout of the place, so I didn't pick much. I started to fret about that quota. I was worried that I was useless. I felt like a dwarf in a swamp. I hadn't seen another worker to talk to or ask advice. One or two had zipped by in their trucks with full crates, chuffed and professional, which made me feel worse. I found my way back to the dock with half a crate and an empty sheet.

"For cryin' out loud, Reilly!" Joe said. "What have you been playing at?"

I rolled my crate off the truck and placed it with the all the others in line.

"I dunno!" I said. I didn't understand how to go any quicker. I handed him my sheet.

"Oh," he said.

"What?"

"You finished. You must have had all the small stuff. You know you worked through your break?"

"I thought we didn't get breaks?"

"Ha!" he laughed. "Of course you get breaks. You just don't get paid for 'em. Go and get a brew."

"Sorry," I said.

I went and found the canteen. I was surprised to see the kitchen open and the place half full of workers doing the other thing. There were dining tables and chairs but also a lounge area with a TV. It was a big outfit. The kitchen was only selling cold sandwiches, the hot food started with breakfast at seven for the real staff. I got a mug of tea and sat on one of the couches next to someone I knew to be Louise Choudhry, Dickie's girlfriend. We hadn't seen each other for a while. I wondered if she'd spoken to Dee, or if they hadn't made up. She nodded to me and said, "Hello, Sean."

"Hello. I thought that was you."

"It still is. Have you just started?"

"Tonight, yes. It's a big place."

"You don't have to clean it," she said as she stubbed out her fag.

"You look good... How've you err... how've you been?"

"Can't talk now." She touched my hand with hers as she got up and went over to one of the dining tables. She rested that same hand on the back of one of the three older women chatting around it. They all stopped talking and looked at me. It was Dickie's ma, Gladys, with Louise's hand on her shoulder.

I gave them a friendly wave and a weak smile. Maybe Gladys is a seen-it, done-it, we all make mistakes kind of person, I thought. She returned a scowl to my half-arsed smile—maybe she's not. She hadn't forgiven me for nearly breaking them up. She obviously liked Louise a lot more than her husband did. I made a mental note to avoid her. Louise kind of waved back though, so I didn't feel too bad, not about us anyway.

They weren't the only ones I knew there. As I was leaving I noticed Dave, the lad. He was sat slumped at a corner table with his eyes closed. It was true Woolies would give anyone a chance. I let him be and snuck on by and went back down to the dock area to get my truck.

Darryl seemed to like my dad. He was trusting him with the deployment of work anyway. We weren't being watched.

"Let's go wild in the aisles!" Joe said as he handed me another pick sheet. "See you for dinner. Two a.m. Keep your ears open for the pips! That means breaktime!" And he gestured to the air and the sounds coming from the radio. He seemed all in love with the place. I hoped it wasn't to be a Gladys night, though, I thought to myself, and the thought I kept to myself for the next few hours as I sped around the warehouse picking myself.

"I was wrong about this place," Joe said. It seemed like we'd be staying on.

After a couple of weeks of loading wagons, we were nearly autonomous. Me and Joe swapped roles regularly to ease the boredom, and because we had been there longest. It gave him more of a physical night and gave me a break. None of the other lads minded; they weren't big on organization maybe. Maybe they liked being pointed in a direction and let go. It also gave some of them other opportunities. There was a lot of thievery. I caught a lad with his hand in the jewelry cage one night. I couldn't do much about it but let the managers know. He hadn't stolen anything; maybe he was just trying it out. Darryl calmly sacked him. Later, when I went to the toilet, I saw the whole place had been trashed. I mean caved in. The lad had taken his rage out on the doors, the walls, and the sinks. There was broken wood floating around, chunks of ceramic all over the place. Maybe he was angry with himself at getting caught, as the mirrors were all smashed too. Dad had been right—there were some dodgy blokes to work within the walls, due to Woolworth's size and need for workers. But it wasn't as bad as all that. Not for us anyway.

The day after the toilet trashing, early in the morning there was a commotion in the loading bay on the back of one of the wagons. I went over to see. Joe was on the tail lift of one of the double-deckers. He was sat slumped on his haunches, rubbing his head; some big boxes lay beside him. A few of the other workers stood around above on the dock. Dave was looking shifty. He'd managed to stick this job and was still here.

"Dad! What happened?"

He didn't answer so I jumped down onto the tail lift.

"Are you okay?"

He looked at me then, but he didn't see me. I lifted him up and pushed the button on the wagon to raise us up.

"There's nowt wrong with him anyway! He should have moved," Dave was saying.

"You probably had your hands in your pockets, you lazy skite!" another lad said.

I walked with Joe over to the gents, but we couldn't even use a sink, as it was still busted, so I took him to the office and sat him down.

"Stay here, Dad. I'll get you a cup of tea."

Joe was still dazed and didn't answer. I went up to the canteen. Darryl was in there with the police, and so I didn't bother him. They had only just gotten 'round to investigating, I guess.

"Wake up, Dad! Drink this."

Joe roused himself and managed the lukewarm brew.

"All right!" he said.

He went back to work. I didn't see where Dave was, skulking in some corner maybe. Joe had already let it go. He never wanted any trouble.

We made full use of the kitchen's breakfast facility after our shift; it was subsidized by the real workers union dues. We had to hang around for an hour after work until they opened up. I don't think the day shift liked us being there, but then we would be shunned by them anyway. I stacked my plate and sat with Joe and ate. Louise was mopping the floor. She found us and sat down also. I introduced them both and continued eating.

"You eat a lot of bacon," Louise said.

"It's purely medicinal," I said.

"Listen... It's my friend's birthday. We're going out early doors, as we have to be back here tonight. You want to come?"

I looked at Joe. He shrugged. "What about Lucy?" I asked him.

"Sure, I'll look after that," Joe said.

"Who's Lucy?" Louise asked.

"None of your business!" he said, giving me a wink.

"No one," I said.

"All right. See you in The Flying Horse at twelve?"

"Okay," I said. "What's your friend's name?"

"Ermm... Sarah..." She got up to go. "Great. I'll see you later."

I was just happy it wasn't Gladys's birthday.

"She's not as nice looking as the other one," Joe said through a mouthful of toast after Louise had gone.

"No," I agreed. "You sure, you'll be okay?"

"Ah, go on!"

The warehouse wasn't far from Tesco, so me and Joe stopped off after our shifty breakfast to use their car park. I practiced some reversing and parallel parking. It came pretty easy after driving those two-gear, idiot trucks.

"I think you're ready," he said.

"I already put in for it, Dad. I've got the test on Friday."

"No kidding."

Even though he'd always been able to drive, he had only become official when Mum kicked him out. He said it gave him more options. He reached into a bag on the back seat and fished out two cans of beer.

"Here! Congratulations! You're a shoo-in!" he said, and we sat there for a few minutes, drinking draughts, watching the sun come up behind the supermarket's massive plastic-lettered horizon.

The Flying Horse Tavern sat patiently tethered, like a good pub, at the foot of the steps leading up to St. Chad's church. I sat inside with a pint of Guinness waiting for Louise. It wasn't sitting well with me. I could taste all the separate parts and I was thinking that all those parts could be broken down further. I could taste too much. Maybe I was just tired. Louise came in and sat next to me at the bar, her eyes were all pupil. She leaned over to hug me. I could taste nothing now but silver. She smelt like Dickie, though. It was a thought that made me laugh.

"Something tickle you?" she asked, but she didn't want

an answer. We had a drink and then she took my hand and led me out of the pub. We climbed the church steps but didn't count them like we all used to on our way to school, then we entered the graveyard and found a place to sit among the headstones.

"Here!" she said and handed me a hip flask. "Mushroom soup." I took a swig. The liquid tasted like pure mud. I gagged a little but swallowed it. "Take another."

"Where did you get this?"

"Eric the Viking. He dries them."

"It's ... disgusting," I said.

She took a swig herself.

"Yes," she said, closing her eyes and holding her nose.

We finished the flask and sat there looking at the clouds and listened to the birds and the town traffic below us.

"How long does it take?"

"I don't know. I've never tried them before." She leaned over and rested herself on me.

"Sean, why did you let everyone believe we slept together?"

"I didn't. I kept saying we didn't. Nobody believed me."

"Well I didn't. Dickie was expecting it of me, I guess. What did he say?"

"He said you were an immoral prick."

"Amoral," I said. "That's what I mean."

"What?"

"He didn't find it too hard to believe that we did."

"No. There was something, though. I didn't mind him believing it," she said. "I thought that some things might be different then, that I might be as well. What a joke that is in this place... Someone like me... Who thought I was different? He didn't, isn't... I guess. We did... the same thing. Not that different. Who is?"

"Right on." I laughed.

"My tongue's numb," she said. "My head!"

"Have you seen Dee recently?"

"No. I guess that's the end of that band. We'll be looking for a new bassist."

"Did she say anything... anything else?"

"We had a whole conversation about snogging toast once. It was funny. I can't remember. Did you see that?" She suddenly pointed up.

It raised my hackles. "What is it?"

I was looking through a glass kaleidoscopic. The grass kept changing colour. The insects in there came out to play, a whole writhing mass of faceless insects in formation. The trees, the trees were better to focus upon, they looked friendly, with big feathery old man faces, Green Man, I guess, or they nodded in the breeze like some granddad in a rocking chair, constantly changing personalities though, with their eyebrows and mouths, mouthing and eyebrowing. And yes! There were the rabbits, or the shapes of rabbits just popping. I saw a giant teddy bear, I did, she didn't. Louise was still here. I remembered her and I forgot her again.

Then we started to walk. There was a bubble around me. Louise was sometimes in it, but I couldn't talk to her and she wasn't listening. Where was she. Where am I. Then we hit Las Vegas, Lancashire. We walked right down the main drag, the strip, there were flashing lights and lasers and whatnot. We saw saw a family of gobl goblins

ins get out of a limousine ine and they kept staring ing and staring at us they had walking sticks ks and were bent double double and had huge noses noses ses I started laughing at them so did Louise. There she is.

There were rushes of panic.

I had been alive for ten minutes.

I had been here for a year.

I had so many thoughts on the tip of my tongue that they flew away like spittle.

He doesn't understand but I know as she cries about it.

I am sorry I say but we've lost her.

An intense heaviness roots me to the ground.

I am bolted down

I cannot move

But I need to cry

I am sat at the feet, the foot, of a giant man.

I have to ask a question...

Why?

I ask him all the questions I can think of.

This giant.

He is ponderous

He knows, and, I'm sure, was going to answer me when he was ready. So I wait.

I find myself lying on the pedestal of John Bright's statue— the one by Thorneycroft in Broadfield Park. He was a wise man, John Bright, was my waking thought. He knows. Immobile, stoic, oh! I don't know if I slept or the fog just cleared. Something does not feel right though. That smell! I remember what it was. I stood up and felt my pants. I realized that I had shat myself. There was a sobering.

I am a mile away from home.

I started walking toward the steps but knew I had to waddle. I got halfway down and saw Louise lying there on the wall; she raised herself when she saw me.

"How are you?" I asked

"How are you?" she said.

She laughed but she didn't look happy. I saw me when I looked at her. She was just another English fucker, working at nothing. And when I helped her get down, she managed to walk but she was waddling too. I liked her right then like I'd never liked anyone, yet I knew I was thinking about someone else.

"There must have been something else in that soup," she said. "What time is it?"

We managed to get a taxi from out front of the town hall. The driver sniffed the air after five minutes.

"Has one of you got dogshit on your shoe?"

"Yes!" I said. "We have."

"Can you feel your fingers?" Louise asked.

It was a profound question. We dropped her off first.

I got home, cleaned up, and crashed into bed.

The cool sheets warmed up quickly, what with all the activity in there. Droplets of aspic sweat tangled in my body hair and grew saw-toothed legs; they burrowed back under my skin through the follicles. They made me twitch and flip like an air-demented fish. I fought them for eye-rolling hours until....

BANG!

The door was getting a beating. We didn't have a doorbell. Our letterbox was being slammed by impatience.

"SEAN! SEAN! WAKE UP!"

I was groggy so it took a while to register. I thought it must be for a different Sean, it couldn't be me. I was the Sean who was sleeping, so it definitely wasn't me they wanted. I'd let the other Sean answer. He went to the door and then I had him go to the toilet for me too so that I could continue with my pillow...Then came the whistling, loud, two-finger whistling that I can't do, shrill and intriguing to my head. I got up and when my body followed we went to the window. Vinny was outside.

"What's up?"

"Get up. You've got to come with me to the hospital!"

"But, I'm fine!"

"Not for you, you tit! It's Joe!" He screamed it so that I would understand.

Vinny drove us up to the infirmary. I was still out of it, but he told me that he had found Joe facedown, floating, in the canal. The dog, Lucy, had made her way home and Sheila wondered why the dog was outside pawing at the door. And then, when there was no answer at our house, Vinny had retraced the dog walk. And well... It was a shock to see a human bobbing about like a bag of rubbish. No offence, he said. I think.

Vinny had fished Joe out and he couldn't do anything, and then he had to leave him on the canal bank to walk back home to phone for help. It was all too late, but they were trying; there was a tremor, a flutter of life left, Vinny said. I was numb.

In the hospital, Dad lay there in the ICU, tubes for the flow in and out of him that they were removing now. I looked at him, pale and vulnerable for once. I had never seen him fully asleep. He looked younger than himself. Had I never seen himself before?

The doctor put his hand on me.

"He's gone," the doctor said. "Do you know what I'm saying to you, Sean?"

"Yes," I said. "Dad's dead."

"Right." Dr. McCauley squeezed me again. "You need to make some phone calls," he said.

I went through Joe's wallet, again, for the last time. I managed to phone his brother, Don. I told him about Dad's delayed concussion and how he'd slipped or tripped and fallen in the canal and been dragged out by a neighbour. How he hadn't made it. Don was in Ireland, so he couldn't come over. He didn't sound surprised at all. He said he'd help from a distance. Then I phoned Errol. Then I phoned a funeral director from a card the Dr. McCauley had given me.

I sat in the waiting room and watched a lamp. It donned a fedora and a raincoat and watched me from its own shadows but eventually settled into itself, into its own essence, and became a flickering lamp again. My arms were jolting under the skin. I had a big stinky tongue that mollusced my palette and wouldn't stop. I couldn't look at a magazine without it looking back at me. I had another call to make that I couldn't, or I could but didn't want to. I had to, though; it was better than this bodyshock. I phoned my mum.

"Mum? It's Sean."

"What do you want?" she said. "Do you need some money? Because I haven't got any."

"No... I don't know... Yes, but... no," I said. "It's Dad."

"What this time?" she said. "He fall over drunk again?"

"Yes. He did." I didn't know how to say any of this. "In the canal this time," I said.

"Well, tell him to dry up!" she said. She laughed herself to tears with that one. She was whooping and gulping and crying down the phone line. I waited for her to stop, as I couldn't get a word in. After that I couldn't bring myself to tell her exactly what happened. Not that it would put a damper on her mood. Her laugh was callous, and I knew she didn't care. But I had to say it.

"He's dead, Mum," I said.

There was a sigh. There was breathing.

"Good riddance," she said. "Sorry, Sean." And there was another breath before the finality of a click and the static buzz of the end of something. I put the phone down on my end, too. Not that I blamed her after all. I don't know why I let her believe that, though, about him being drunk again. I should have told her about the concussion, the reason. I should have told her about the end. It wasn't his fault. He was only walking a dog; maybe it was the dog's fault.

Errol was waiting there behind me. "Don't worry about it," Errol said. "Come on, I'll give you a lift."

As we were driving back, Errol said to me, "You know, I heard you on the phone."

"Yeah?"

"Why didn't you tell her that it was an accident?"

"I don't think she'd care," I said.

"Maybe not... but it's all he's got left."

"What? There is nothing. He's gone."

"But he was doing something. He changed. He was helping you."

"She doesn't care, though," I said. "He could never change what he did to her."

"No," Errol agreed. "But... He wasn't that guy anymore."

"What guy?" I asked. "It's hard to be the wife beater when you're divorced."

"Sean," Errol said, "he was nothing but good to you, and you know it. I'm going to miss him. We're all going to miss him, no matter what he did."

"Mum won't miss him."

"Don't be so sure about that," Errol said.

And as we drove back down to our house, I thought of it as just a little box of made-up memories. I hated the box. We were all just in boxes.

Errol came inside the house with me, but I didn't really care. I started to throw stuff as soon as I got in the door. Any photograph I could find I tore up. I was punching the walls as he got hold of me.

"Sit down, shithead," Errol said and threw me down on the couch. He got some of the poitin from the sideboard and poured it into two of my dad's Waterford crystal tumblers. The only translucent collection!

"Do you want to know the last thing he said to me?" Errol said, as I calmed down. "It's a good one." He drank.

"Sure." I shrugged. So Errol spoke.

"Joe said that the previous week as he was driving home that he felt really bad because—he had told no one—he ran over an animal... (Errol drank) ...Joe felt the unnatural bump in the road, as his vehicle left the firmament and then came crashing back down to earth. And when he parked, stopped, he got out to take a look and went back and saw the twitching thing, it looked like a rabbit, and he felt bad for the little fella. As he was bent there in the road, wondering what to do, another car stopped—to ask if he was okay—so Joe explained the situation to the driver and the driver of the other car said, 'Okay! Maybe I can help!' and then, this other driver went back to his car and rooted around in his boot, really dug in there, chucked stuff about and then, then he came back to Joe, he came back with... with a can or a bottle or something, smiled at Joe, shook the canister in his face, muttered some mumbo jumbo and then sprayed the wounded, twitching mammal, gave it a wet silhouette on the asphalt. There was a small pause before the animal hopped up and ran off into the bushes— as if nothing had happened, business as usual—and well he, Joe, was gobsmacked, and after a, after a, after an hiatus, he had to ask the other driver, 'That was marvelous! What was that?' And the other driver had his own small pause before he answered, 'Hair restorer.'"

Errol laughed and roused me. I didn't laugh; I hadn't heard it before, but I couldn't. Errol laughed at the idiocy of the story. He laughed at his own telling of it. He laughed because Joe had told it to him. He laughed for Joe and the sharing.

I can't remember my dad's last words to me. They're in there somewhere, so these can be my dad's last words—

"Hair restorer"—out loud, anyway. He wouldn't laugh anymore neither.

Errol dropped me off. I had work to do. I got home and didn't even open the door. I got in our car instead and turned the ignition and then sat there and thought about it. Two miles was easy enough. I put on a cassette. I sang my head off to some Jesus and Mary Chain and drove. But I couldn't drown anything out. It was my first night at work without him. I hadn't thought of that. I hadn't thought of all he'd done for me recently until Errol mentioned it. Why had Joe done that now? I sang my head off as I drove up Halifax Road on my own. And yet Errol's words came back and made sense to me. Joe had been trying to make things better, in his own remorseful, guilty way. He knew that he was a fuck-up but I could never guess to how he felt about what he'd done to my mum, beating her up as he did, and ruining our happy life together, because he had to shut that part of himself down, just to get on. That was a joke anyway, happy life. Her black eyes were the punchline. And everyone in the family knew, but nobody laughed, even though he could still tickle them. I could never understand anything he ever did now he was gone. I was upside down. And I had to get on.

I parked outside the warehouse and went into work and clocked Joe and me in. We had done it before for each other. No one was ever there before us. A few of the deadheads maybe, but they came and went. No one knew that. I wasn't going to tell anyone that Joe was no more.

"Where's Joe?" Darryl asked.

"He's in the bog," I said.

I started telling the lads what trucks to take and handed out some pick sheets after the others turned up.

Darryl came by later and saw everything was going swimmingly with the orders for the night. He didn't even ask where Joe was again. So I was Joe now, I had to remember, I was Joe, and I was me. I had him down. I did it all week. I clocked us both in and I got all the timesheets signed and I collected the cash. I would work nights and sleep during the day. And the next week, I did it again.

It gave us enough to pay back Errol for the cremation.

***

"We're nuns."

I am on a boat full of them.

Novices anyway, is what they tell me. Out of habit.

I haven't had sex for a month, I am thinking, me too. But I was making polite chat when I asked what they all did for a living...

The novices had been noisy and full of themselves, and I was a party to it by proximity. We were sat on the floor together because the ferry was so busy that all the seats had been given up to the infirm. It was a choppy crossing. Nuns? They shut me down with that shocker so I contented myself with a can of beer. One of them wanted a quieter word though. She waited for the attention to tangent itself before she isolated me.

"What's the matter?" she asks.

"Not much." I lift up the urn and show her. "Ash! No matter really, just my dad."

I'm drunk and she knows.

"He needs an introduction," I say, as I pat the urn, to make her feel more included.

"I'm Fiona, pleased to meet you," she says, shaking the urn like a hand.

"This is Joe." I put him to my ear. "He likes your freckles."

There's a silence, as that was a bit weird of me.

"You going to drink all of those?" She points out the case of Stella I had purchased from the duty free.

"Not possible. Would you like one?"

"Mm!"

I offer what I am cradling to her friends then. "You?"

Her girlfriends decide I'm not worth the bother. They see no potential in me, but they take a can each anyway.

"Don't you think you've had enough?" Fiona says.

"Not yet."

"How would you know?"

"I wouldn't."

"When do you stop?"

"When I do."

"Does it hurt?"

"Doesn't everything?"

"No. He heals. He's there for you." I don't know if she's having me on.

"He's there for you," I say.

"All of us."

"How would you know?"

"Because he is."

"Just because?"

"Yes," she says.

"I've been godless since I was eight. But I only started

drinking when I was fourteen. Do you want a beer?"

I drink some as she shakes her head.

"We've just come from a choir competition, in Liverpool."

"How was that?"

"We won, thanks for asking!"

I see a unity in them, a sureness, they're a big-toothed grin of a team.

"Well done." I drink.

"We're celebrating."

"Doesn't look like it," I say.

"You don't have to get... listen.... Come with me."

So I go with her; I have to take my dad, up the carpeted stair onto the top deck. She holds the urn while I pull at the wind-stuck, leaden door. We look out for a while. The whole world is dark silver. Then, there, in the howl, and staring at the waves in the dark, she kisses me. I don't know why.

"Where are you going?" Fiona asks me, even as I stand there this close to her.

"I'm taking him back."

"Home." She flexes her neck.

"Yes."

I put the urn down between my feet so that I can free my hands. She kisses me more.

We promise each other some sunrises as we see the land we look for. She glows in the beauty of the morning. It must feel good to be going home, to belong. It's my first time here in years. I suddenly feel like a tourist in a familiar place that has grown without me. I break away from her and apologize.

We just stand there, in our own wake. It's awkward. She starts to shift from foot to foot after a while.

"It was nice meeting you."

"It was nice meeting you."

She goes back down to find her coven as we dock.

I give everyone some space, the last on deck again. When I descend it is through some squegging emotions. I know that they weren't nuns, and that they've drunk all my beer. My dad rolls about the ship in his new plastic house, laughing his lid off.

Disembarked, I stand in line at border security. There are kids and patient mothers all around me. I have nothing to declare. I get to the front of the queue. A uniformed lady, sardined into her seat, beckons me.

"What's in the bag?"

"My dad," I answer.

"Open it!"

I remove some socks and y-fronts from the bag, take the urn out and hand it to her. She gets hold of it and reads the details, stuck there on a tatty piece of paper.

"Death certificate?"

I have that too and produce it.

"Good luck," she says, unsmiling. "Move along."

I shoulder the bag and carry on. The arrival hall is a riot of meeting; there are wholesome tears on happy cheeks. There is no greeting for me. It's still just us for a while. I have him yet.

We crawl up and onto a bus to the city centre.

"Come on!" I say, to no one in particular. We sit upstairs and jig up and down like memories in an addled brain. He starts talking to me.

"Where are we off to?"

"Did you never go to Dublin?"

"I've been twice, no three times, four now."

"What did you do?"

"Well. It was the gateway. It was the cheapest and quickest way to get out. To escape."

"From what?"

"You'll see."

I wondered on that. "For you, though, Dad?"

"For me... Yeah!"

I remembered the way Joe used to sigh then. He did this intake of breath sometimes on the word 'yeah.' A gasp he sucked back in. A memory not allowed to depart, some gas trapped, a bubble corked. His whole resting life, his resignation was a sigh; it was an inward 'yeah.'

"The first time I was in Dublin, we were passing through from Cork. I was helping a girl get over to Liverpool for an abortion. Afterwards I sent her home and stayed in England. My family changed towards me after that one. I just waved Ireland goodbye."

"Why would you do that? Who was it?"

"Because I had to... And I was the only one that had the money. She was a good friend. Back then anyways."

We get near St. James's Gate and I can smell that chocolate malt roast on the air.

"There was a time when we were together, all of us. When we enjoyed each other's company and we were young and free—not free in a money way but more a wild way where we gamboled in the fields carelessly. Do you remember, Dad?"

"No! Did we? I must have forgotten the good times."

"Well, maybe you weren't there, just Mum, do you think?"

"I doubt it. She never gamboled in her life."

"Didn't she?"

"Did she ever? She married me."

There was that waft again that wakes me from my idiot reveries. I don't like chocolate, but I can understand the fondness for Guinness. I feel great as we get off the bus to face the day. I wonder if I should leave some of him here, scatter him about a bit, but I'm not asking him.

We wander through the grey granite of the city and hardly look up. I think we need a drink, or some breakfast of some kind. There's only unleavened bread on offer at the moment though. I watch the mud of the Liffey swirl above secrets and as we wait for noon, I think on which is moving slower—time or the river or my metabolism. We made it out of England at least, but that sea that we both crossed is still there. I'm still here.

We eventually get over to Poolbeg Street, into Mulligan's. I place the urn on the bar and we get into it. I order two pints.

"What are we doing here?" Joe says.

"We're on our way. You told me about this place, remember? You said it was one of Joyce's favourite pubs."

"True! Although he did bugger off. For better wines and freedom. Anyway, that was two lifetimes ago. Well, you could leave me here I guess."

"He found freedom and Nazis, and the wines."

"And the women... I don't want to go back here, Sean."

"You have to. I promised Don, and he promised your mum."

"But I didn't."

"Well. You don't get a choice now. You're dead."

"And whose fault is that?"

"I don't know, Dad. Dave's fault maybe? Lucy's? How can you blame a dog?" I say. "What does it matter where you are?"

"I guess it doesn't. I always wanted to be scattered in the Mediterranean. To float like a dirty old man on the tits of Europa."

"Well that's not happening," I say. "I've got enough money to get you home and me back again."

We get some peppery eggs on cremated toast smeared with gorgonzola, oh, and we watch as a family of German tourists approach the bar. I scoot my dadbag a little closer to me, as he is taking up too much room on his perch.

Their own paterfamilias is tall and clean with a big blond moustache. They could be Swedish or Swiss, what do I know.

"Three pints of Guinness please!" the blond gentleman orders.

"How old?" shoots back the barman.

"Excuse me?"

"How old is the kid?" the barkeep points to the teenage son trying to hide behind his mother.

"Ah, sixteen years old."

"So, that's two pints and a coke is it?" says the barman.

My dad lets out a chortle; he doesn't snicker, never did. It's more of a loud expulsion most times. Or was it me?

"What are you laughing at?" a different barman rounds on me. "Who served you? Show me some ID!"

"I would if I could find it." I poke in our bag. "It's kind of deep... down...in...there."

The barman doesn't blink so I take out my driving license. He grunts.

A man in a suit moves next to me at the bar then. He has a face that looks beaten but not freshly.

"All right? I 'eard your accent. You're from my neck of the woods. I'm Nigel."

I hear his accent too. He's from Manchester.

"Thereabouts," I say. "Sean," I say and shake his hand. "What's up?" I ask.

"Not a lot. What you doin' 'ere? Got family?"

"I do. I'm here with my dad." I pat the bag.

"Right." He's not that interested. "Listen, you got any gear?"

"Naw!" I say, "I just got off the ferry."

"You want some?"

It's a bit early, I think, but I say, "Why, what have you got?"

"All sorts."

"I don't like licorice," I mutter, but he heard me.

"Nice one, funny lad. Stick with me. We've got a party tonight. Buy us a drink and I'll sort you out."

So I do. I buy Nigel a drink. What the fuck, I think. My dad just died, and I could do with some mental release because all I'm hearing is Joe's voice.

"Sean, don't...please?"

But I don't answer to Joe anymore. I stop listening to him and the next thing I know, he's gone again.

***

"SON?"

I try to talk but cannot. I wake up in a different country with two women poking me. "Son? What are you doing here?"

That is what comes through, after a while. My head is stuck to the table. I'm in a pub. I can tell by the smell.

"What day is it?" I ask.

"What sort of question is that?"

"I don't know."

"CHEWS-ADAY! Where are you usually on Chews-aday?"

"Which one?" I say, biding time, blinking.

"Okay," she says. "Would you like a calendar?"

"Were you with the party last night?" the other woman says.

I nod.

"It's okay, he was at the do. Just give him some tea. I think he's from Your-Up."

I drink a cup of sugary tea and rouse from the snug as they tidy around me.

"Did you see the foot lady yesterday, Maisie?"

"I did, Min. I have to say, I had my doubts but I've no complaints."

"These big-city blow-ins. They don't know what we have to put up with."

"Oh, now! Her mother was a culchie, just like you."

"There she was hacking away at me foot, like a combine harvester. I says to her it's not that kind of corn!"

As I listen to this, am I forgetting something? I can't feel my fingers. What is it that I had? I had something with me, I know. I can yawn. I can't taste my tongue. I had a tongue with me last time I looked. Who looks at their tongue? I can't feel my bag. That's it! I had a bag with me and something to do with it. And then I remember my dad.

"Where's my bag?" I can't shout, as my head... but the ladies are hovering nearby. I feel vertiginously sick, so I scuttle off to the bog. I'm not sure I'm going to be able to piss, though, as my dick has shrunk and I can't find it. My whole body turns cold. I pull down my jeans and sit on the toilet and vomit into the sink next to my head. I start to sweat and the convulsions help me release some urine, and watery shit. Everything is all right after ten minutes, except that my arse and my throat are sore. I wash my face and drink from the bathroom tap. It tastes like cold tarn water. And I am grateful for that time left alone. When I come out of there, the ladies are polishing the brass pipes of the beer pumps. I sit back down and stew. They leave me be. But when I eventually ask, no bag has been lost here, or found.

I think I know what has happened. Nigel took me to a party, a wake, and we drank and got shit faced, and what was it we took? Acid maybe. I know that he took my bag, too, and I'll never find him... and I am a fool full of regret that cannot function until I get more sleep. I nod off again, but I am in and out of things. Many demons grin in my face. What can they really do to me now except gloat? Fuck them, I say and drift off.

As soon as the float hits the cash register my eyes pop open. I have a little money still tucked into my socks and I make my way to the bar.

"So?" the barmaid asks.

"A pint of diesel, please."

"What's up with you?"

"I lost my dad."

"Uh-huh!" She's listening. "Have you phoned anyone?"

"It's not like that. He was in an urn," I say.

"Well. Okay... Where did you last see him? Sorry, but...," she says matter of factly.

"Dublin," I say. And she laughs at that. She snorts a big one and curses and crosses herself to keep the demons at bay. "Holy Feckin' Jeezus! Do you even know where ye are?"

"No," I say.

"Well, I hope you said your goodbyes!" she says and tuts at me.

"Yeah," I say. "Not really. I wasn't there for him. It was an accident."

"Here," she says and hands me the remote for the TV. "I'll talk to you in a bit. You're in Wicklow."

"Thanks," I say.

She goes then and busies herself with her rigamarole, leaving my pint to settle into itself. I don't blame her. I'm a mess and she knows. I put my head down on the bar and wonder about the virtues of wood versus brass for a pillow.

"I'm Sharon," she shouts.

"Sean," I say back to the shout.

"Dublin!" she laughs. "Sorry!"

Eventually, the stout burns my throat, but I don't care. I run to the toilet again and I think that should be the end of it. I drink some more after and am able to keep it down. I weigh the consequences and wonder whether this has happened before. The stealing of an urn, I mean. It must have happened before. Maybe Nigel thought there was something else in it? Something smuggled and illicit? He mustn't have believed me. I still have the death certificate, too, so Nigel is obviously not a good thief, just some opportunist. Where does that leave me?

I sit there sipping and feel sorry for myself. A few more patrons enter the pub. They say hello to me but I am lost. Sharon is on the phone for a bit but comes back. "Okay." She lights a fag and blows the smoke out of the side of her mouth and picks a piece of tobacco out of her teeth, I guess, it could be something else. "So, what are you going to do?"

"Can I get one of those?" I ask, pointing to her fag.

"No." She considers. "You have to earn it." She gives me a hard stare. "You were a dick last night apparently." She blows more smoke. "But funny. Keiran let you stay so I guess you're okay."

I am feeling hungry now with my emptied belly. I look about the bar, but they don't have much. "Can I have a pickled egg please?"

"Sure," says Sharon. "It's your funeral.... Sorry!"

"I like them," I say. I tuck into it. It's like a chemistry lesson exploding in my mouth, but it helps with my reality, it gives me a jolt. "Will you let me collect glasses for you tonight?" I ask, cheeks full of acidic protein. "Then I can earn it."

Sharon thinks. "Why not?" She puffs. "But I tell you,

there's not much going on." She gives me one of her cigarettes. I agree with her, but I have a lot going on. I have to get to Cork for the funeral. And I have no remains to bury. Where is it? You, I mean? You could be anywhere. I need some air. I venture out into Ballythisorthat. My head is clear as a hangover. The sky has rainclouds, which helps my blinking eyes. There is not much to this main street, but I am stood next to the train station. Ah, yes. Bray. We came on the train, a bunch of us. It's not far at all. I wander down the drag to sit and crash on forgotten sand. I light the cigarette and have an idea that filters through the memories of the bar, the grey sky, sounding gulls, the shick and shuck of a sea that we'd skimmed thin stones at, that sea between us that was so easy to cross. I have an idea that filters through our history of you and me. We were terrible. Most things didn't matter. I have an idea as ash drops onto and into and through the stones. You are gone and I need to find you back there.

I return to the pub.

"How are you, Sean?" comes the cry. There are faces becoming more familiar by the minute.

"I'm fine. I'm fine." I stumble back to the bar.

"Sharon can I have the whole jar of eggs please? And another pint."

"Where are you going with this?" she asks, but she gives me the jar. The weight and size of it are comparable to the urn you were in. Of course it's glass and not plastic, I'll have to explain something but not that I haven't got you. And there are only ten eggs left. "It's doable!" I say to Sharon.

"Sure. Weirdo!" she says.

"Okay, everyone, the pickled eggs are on me! Do it for the old feller!" I shout and raise the jar aloft with both hands like I've just won the cup. I hear one whoop and I have a few takers, but I have to eat most of the eggs myself. It's a chastening experience. I know I can throw them away, but it's a waste. I probably won't eat for a while anyway. My stomach revolts a little, but I manage. Afterward, I take the jar to the jacksy and I rinse out the glass, clean off the label, and then take it back in and let it dry on the bar. I tip things in my favour.

All night I collect empties for my new friends and clean out the ashtrays, only I keep all the ash in the old pickle jar. I get a few free pints out of it and feel a lot steadier about my person. Later, I do have to sift it a little, but at least I have a new dad, although he's lost weight. I wander down to the sea again and mingle some of the red sand with the grey ash. There he is now, all ready to go home and waiting to be interned. He smells of vinegar and old smoke, but he would anyway. I tighten the lid and stick on a new label that I made up on him from some paper and tape. I have Wednesday to get across country. I fall asleep on the same snug couch cradling the new urn.

***

The Cork train arrives and I get off it. I have a new shirt on now and so my dad, Joe, has a new bag, red and plastic with the clothes shop's name emblazoned in gold letters above the words "CRAZY SALE."

Except that Joe's not in there. I don't know where he's gone.

I don't even know where his ashes are. I lost him.

All that is in the bag is an old pickled egg jar full of cigarette ash and sand from a pub near Bray in County Wicklow.

Don is there to meet us at the train.

"Jesus, Sean!" he says when he sees me. It seems like an age before he offers his hand to shake. "C'mon."

We head off in his Toyota.

"You look a lot bigger since I last saw you."

"I've grown."

"And what's with your hair?"

"It grew, too."

"Well, we have a pair of shears at home that'll sort you out. And you could do with a shower."

I look down at my feet. I should have bought some fresh socks.

"Sorry," I offer.

"There's a smell coming off you that would pickle a rock."

That's not me, I'm about to say. "A shower, yeah, thank you." I shut up.

Aunt Maureen is standing in the driveway. I always call her that; even my dad called her that, like she has first two names, Aunt Maureen. I clamber out.

"Hello, Sean." She pecks me on the cheek. She's a tall lady and I can see eye to eye with her now. "Look at the cut of you!"

"It's a cut he's needing," Don says.

Aunt Maureen looks like she's about to tousle my hair

but she folds her arms across herself and I see her look down at the plastic carrier I'm holding. She looks back up at me then turns and walks to the house. "A cup of tea?" she shouts at the pebble-dashed wall.

"C'mon, son. And I'll find you something better to carry that... carry him in," Don says.

I'm in my cousin Anthony's room. He's left a few clothes behind, so I nab some clean underwear after my shower. The rest of the stuff is sports gear, and I'm not wearing his bloody tracksuit, so I put my black jeans back on. Joe is on the desk there now in a white canvas bag. He's moved house quite a few times for a dead feller. Except it's not him, I remember. Maybe I should just think that way though. It would make it more convincing, I tell myself. They haven't asked to look anyway. I go down for tea.

"How's the egg and chips, Sean?" Aunt Maureen asks.

"Eloquent," I say.

"What's that?" says Don.

"Fine, thanks," I say. "They're speaking to me."

"Another smart arse!" Don says, so I change the subject to his idiot son.

"How's Anthony doing?"

"Grand. He's working in a bar in New York. Ten dollars a night just to show up! Illegal like, but they don't care. He gets his tips ... Here!" Don gets up and lifts a postcard from the fridge.

It has an old photo of Brendan Behan with Harpo Marx at a party in New York. They are both wearing curly wigs and Behan is honking a car horn into Harpo's ear. Harpo is doing a clown face. I turn the card over. HAVING A BLAST THE GUINNESS IS SHITE! LOVE ANTO.

"Sounds like he's enjoying himself... I'd go and visit if I had the money."

"Oh, he'll be back before you know it," Aunt Maureen says. "Probably get thrown out on his thick ear." She laughs and Don joins in.

"Yeah, anyway, you have to be twenty-one over there, Seany. You can't be having any fun over there until you're twenty-one!" he says.

"Well. I have a job anyway," I say.

Aunt Maureen perks up. "Have you now? Tell us all about it."

"Well. It's not that interesting really."

"What job is?" says Don. "That's why it's called a job. Now, a career, that's an animal of an altogether different feather."

"Shush, Don! Let Sean tell us."

"I'm the shop steward on the nightshift in the main hub warehouse for Woolworth's North West," I lie.

"That's a grand title." Don laughs loud at that one. He snorts. He gets hysterical, and it's contagious. Aunt Maureen guffaws herself.

"Oh, Don. Stop. You've embarrassed him," she says.

"Sorry, Sean. It's just... how did that come about?" he asks.

"Well it was Dad's position really. I just filled in, as I'd been there longest apart from him. No one else knew the ropes. It just sort of evolved after his accident."

"Oh. Sure. I see."

We finish our meal then in the growing quiet, some words taking longer to disappear from the room. I get up and take the plates to the kitchen and start to wash them. Aunt Maureen comes in after me.

"He didn't mean anything. You know. He was only kidding you on."

I shrug and look her in the eye.

"If you want, we'll take you to The Donny for a pint. You've had a bit of a trek."

"Sure."

"Maybe you should brush your hair first though." She makes a move toward me, but again takes her hand back and folds her arms across her body. "And wear one of Anthony's jackets, the blue one on the back of the door. It's cold out."

In the pub Don has a hold of my shoulder at the bar.

"None of us got on with Joe, not even Ma, but we're sorry for you, Sean. And we'll be glad to be done with this ... thing tomorrow." Don gestures at the canvas bag I have brought with me to the pub and placed between us on a bar stool. "You're always welcome here though... I think." Don belches a stout belch.

"Thanks," I say. "I could have done this in Rochdale, you know. He had friends."

"No. No. Your auld Granny, god bless her, she made a promise he... we, would all be buried here. God willing. It's just a shame we had to... you know..."

"Cremate?" I ask.

"Yes... I mean, it is a lot cheaper! But the auld ones don't like it." He nudges me, takes a sip, and then brightens.

"So. What have you been up to, apart from being the King of Woolworth? Ha ha!" He giggles into his pint then, slaps it on to the bar. It takes him a while to get over his own mirth.

"Have you a girlfriend?" he asks me.

"There was. Dee," I lie. "I haven't really been thinking about her though, with all this."

"How do you mean? She's not there for you, huh?"

"Oh, no! Sure. Wild mushrooms couldn't drag her away. I just, you know... I need some space."

"I know what you're saying... I think." Don shakes his head. "So, it's not the main thing at the moment," he says. "Do you want a game of pool? Or darts, mebbe? Huh? Darts, is it?" He flicks his head over at the board. I guess he likes darts.

"I'm not playing for money," I say.

"No, right enough. C'mon then!"

I grab hold of new dadbag, tuck him under my armpit, and we walk over to the dartboard. Aunt Maureen is talking to her friend Eileen in a snug close by.

"Hello, Sean. Are we all grown up now, are we?" Eileen says.

"Hello, Aunt Eileen. Can I get you a drink?"

"Oh! I wouldn't consider it. And don't call me that."

"Sorry." I grin, and she laughs at me.

Eileen says to Aunt Maureen, "He's offering us a drink with his dad in a bag, tucked underneath his arm, like Don used to do with Joe's head, do you remember, Mo?" Eileen finds it funny but in some way that makes her shudder.

Aunt Maureen is nodding at that memory of the brothers, but she isn't laughing.

"What are you carrying that thing about with you for anyway?" Eileen says to me. "It's not right, you know. He should've been buried." She continues, "There are laws in this country that you English don't even care about."

"Shush, Eileen!" Aunt Maureen says. "It's not Sean's

fault."

"It's my dad, Eileen. I was just giving him his last pub crawl. We'll bury him. Don said we can." And I know it isn't him, my dad, under my arm, but it is now. I know it, I'm thinking what I have now here is him. This is it. I want to scatter him all in their faces right now, but I hold on. "It's all I could do really. I couldn't ship a body," I say.

Aunt Maureen changes the subject then. "Here, I'll get them," she says, and she hands me a tenner.

"Only a half for me, thanks," Eileen says with a dismissive flick of a gaudy baubled finger.

"So I'll get them then," I say and I walk off to the bar again. But as I go, I turn sharply to say my thanks for the drink, as I'd forgotten, and I see Eileen look at Aunt Maureen and they are both shaking their heads and snapping at each other about something and they don't consider me there at all.

"Joe!" I say.

Joe Sullivan, the barman, says, "What can I get you?"

"Three pints and half a Harp," I order. "Joe, do remember my dad, Joe?" I lift up the canvas-wrapped jar and plop it back onto the bar.

"I never forget a face," he says. And how we laugh about that.

After one game of arrows with Don, I want to sit down. It's winner stays on, so he has to play Graham Whatshisface that I just met. I go back over to Aunt Maureen and she makes room for me. There is something different about her now, or maybe it's me.

"Come here, Seany!" she says, all aglow. I sit next to her and she grabs a hold of me and rubs my hair and pinches my cheeks. I don't know why it's taken her so long, but she has tears in her eyes and doesn't say another word. Eileen strokes Aunt Maureen's arm then and we sit about in the silence between us again although we can hear Don's roars from behind as he punctuates every thunk of every dart himself, in either small victory or minor setback.

"Listen to that eejit!" Aunt Maureen says into her drink and then she flips as she notices the canvas bag I have put between us. She yells, "Get that fucking thing off me!"

And the human hubbub of the pub gets sucked down the stunned plughole, yet there is still sound, a few gurgles and a "What the feck?" from a dark corner. And there are echoes of words that ring as a shrill gong's farewells, because home here is a dead man, *that ... fucking... thing...* he would be laughing right now, in the face of family, and I can hear his voice ringing. And I want to hear him. All those stories he'd told me about this lot and their values, and how unfaithful they were to them. How high and mighty they could be and how small they made him feel. All those stories that he passed on were what I believed. Echoes. Ringing. And I hate Aunt Maureen as much as he used to right now. Or at least as much as I used to think he did. My brain is on fire and I want to yell and I want to punch a wall. But I don't; I breathe because this is not my place. Then the static subsides as Don comes over.

"What's the matter?" Don asks.

"Sorry," I say and remove Dad and place him between my feet on the floor.

"That's where he should be... Under fucking ground," Aunt Maureen says shaking and vehement.

But the fire has not left me either.

"Why did my Dad leave here?" I ask Don.

"I guess he didn't like us that much...." He sighs and squeezes into the seat next to me.

"No, Don," Aunt Maureen butts in.

"It's not Sean's fault, Mo!" Don says to her, before turning back to me. "No. It's not that he didn't like us. It's not a question of that, Sean... Or maybe it is. We all just didn't get on. He could be terrible and we could too. Do you know what I'm getting at?"

"No," I say and I take another drink from my pint. "Why? What happened?"

"It's to do with your Aunt Maureen's friend, a long time ago."

"You mean the one who got the abortion?"

"Jesus Christ!" Aunt Maureen splutters. "He told you about that."

"Someone did, once, I can't remember." I watch them.

Don and Eileen exchange glances. Eileen looks worried, but Aunt Maureen is looking right at me.

"What else do you know, you little shite? What else did he tell you?" she is screaming at me now. "Wipe that smile off your face!"

"I know it was you," I guess.

I finish my drink but as I put the pint glass down on the table I sense something coming toward me, a fast-moving presence that, before I can blink or look up, makes contact with my head. The force is from above and makes me nod down sharply, so that my chin hits my chest, before my neck cracks back again. It's like I've cleared the ball with a header from a volley, but 10 yards away and backward. I can hear bubbles popping inside of my ears, and I can feel a heat throughout my skull, but I cannot see or comprehend much. I still have the glass clutched in my hand and I concentrate on sliding it away from me across the wet tabletop so that my face does not land on it. I look up and see Aunt Maureen standing over me with a vicious look on her face and an ashtray in her hand; she's rearing back, ready to hit me again. And I think I should keep a hold of the glass, but my grip loosens as electric shocks shoot through my arm and fingers. Don has pinned my arm to the table so that my fist unclenches. There are sounds, shouts, as others rush about the place. I can't fall, as I'm sitting with my back against the wall. The next blow knocks me sideways though. The ashtray has smacked into my cheek and I slump horizontal down to the floor as something else, a shiny boot, quickly pushes my nose into my face. The sharpness of that pain stings and makes my eyes water and rouses me a little. I struggle to get up but then I don't bother. I see other people above me grabbing and hitting each other, the whole place is a riot of shuffling feet and dust from my vantage point. I give in. I just wrap my arms around my head and curl into a ball.

When I come to, I am in a white room, a bloody hospital. I can smell it, the bleach and the piss underneath. I feel awful. I feel like my brain has been replaced by a trapped sparrow and my mouth is inside out. Eventually I press a button for a nurse. She is sat in a room down there. I see a light come on and she busies herself and comes out of the door toward me. She's smiling and has big teeth. Geraldine is the name on her badge.

"Sean!" she says. "You're awake. How are you feeling?"

"Where's my bag?"

"It's with your stuff."

"Where's that?"

"It's here. Don't worry. How are you feeling?"

"Thirsty."

"Will you be wanting some Lucozade?" she asks.

"Sure."

She leaves me then. All I can tell is that it is late. She comes back.

"There you are." She gives me a drink. "The police are wanting to talk to you. He's been waiting." She indicates with her head toward the door.

"Okay then," I say. "Wait though. What happened to me? Why am I here?"

"Let's have a look at you... Stitches!" she says. "In the head ... and the cheek. We couldn't give you anything, as you had enough booze in you to tranquilize a horse, so! Welcome back to the world... Have you a headache now?"

"I feel a little numb," I say.

"I'll get you something for the pain," she says and bustles away in her crinoline.

"Sean Reilly?" the Gardai says.

"Yes, officer." I sit up a bit and try to look presentable. The drugs are kicking in—I don't know what Sister Geraldine gave me, but I like it and I'm slurring yet I could care less and it all helps with confidence; I think these things, anyway.

"How are you feeling, son?"

"I don't know... Bad?" I don't know why I'm asking

him. He's a small feller. He takes his hat off and sits on the end of my bed.

"Sorry!" he says, shuffling his bum.

It doesn't matter much to me; my feet don't reach the end of the bed anyway.

"I've some bad news for you," he says, his pale-blue eyes refusing to meet mine. "I have to arrest you."

"Okay," I say. I don't care. "What for?"

"Oh, it's just a formality. You were unconscious before, so. The thing is you started an affray in a public place."

"I did?" I ask.

"That's what the witnesses say, yes," he says. "But... don't fret too much. I've heard that we'll be willing to drop the charges. If you just go home."

"Home?" I ask. And I wonder where that is.

"Yes..." and he sucks his teeth now. "Yes... your family, your Aunt Maureen, they request it. They don't want a fuss."

"What does that mean?" I ask.

"I have to escort you to the airport," he says.

"Oh!" I feel weird and bad that he has to take me to the airport. I haven't even got a ticket. "Sorry," I say again. "But hold on!" Things are coming back to me. "What about Dad? What about the funeral?"

"Just calm down. It'll be okay, Sean. You just have to leave. There'll be no funeral. Your family scattered the ashes in the river," he says.

It's a joke. The river flows out to sea, away from this place. What was the point of bringing him back? And yet it wasn't him anyway and I want to laugh at that but I can't because I was supposed to be taking care of him, Joe. I was supposed to bring him home. Yet I knew that he never wanted to come. And then I realize that I even failed at the pretense of all of this. I just fucked it all up again. And before the officer can tell me anything else I start to cry. And I can't help it, but I turn into my pillow then and I let it all go. I sob. I sob and I wail. He gets off the bed. I can feel the pressure release. Then I can hear myself howl and suck air like the baby I am; I cry and cry but there is no comfort, not even when Nurse Geraldine comes back.

"I only came here because of them," I say.

"He's just upset is all," she says to the officer. "Now, now!" she says to the back of me. "All will be well."

"Will it?" I say. "Will it."

DOGHOUSE

"It's a big house, you can't miss it." My legal aid solicitor, Mr. Barnes, had said that, but still I can't seem to find it, this big house that will be my new home. The night is dark, obviously, and the road is slick, and the drizzle in the air doesn't know whether to find land or cloud, but the rain is constant, so constant and light and indecisive that the streetlamps cannot help with direction, just some comfort in the gloom. My eyes are giving up and my hair is a mess. My cloth bag is stuck to my shoulder. I am panicking a little about the time, as my train was late and I don't know where I am exactly and I have no watch. What's a watch?

Mr. Barnes gave me the address and some petty cash, but it didn't stretch to a taxi. My boots are old and every step I take squeezes more water from my already rotten socks.

Where is this place? Trinity Road, number 52. It can't be far, the bus driver said it was just around the corner from the shops. They are all closed now. There are shutters to deflect any attention.

There it is then, looming, my new home, all lit and drizzled. I made it with a couple of hours to spare, after all my panic. I let out some breath and declench my teeth and knock, and knock. I realize there is a bell and push it.

A man with a head like a shelled walnut answers the door; he has a pipe dangling from one of the many nooks on his face.

"Are you the warden?" I ask.

The Walnut's face cracks and adds some more creases.

"No, mate! In there!" He points his pipe over his shoulder toward a door marked "WARDEN."

And then there I am, dripping, in the office, as the bald, bearded Warden tickles some paperwork inside a very thin folder that gives in easily and laughs my particulars into my face.

"Sean Reilly, No Fixed Abode, Charged with Theft. You've been placed in the custody of the Probation Service until your sentencing. Is that correct?" The Warden's voice is slow with flatter vowels than mine, but I understand him.

"Yeah," I say. He gives me a look. Am I supposed to say sir? I am all dressed in black and my hair is plastered to my head. I know what he's thinking...

"Are you on drugs?" Well, I didn't think he was thinking that. I thought he was thinking I was someone else…

"No," I say, sitting up. "I'm just tired."

He goes back to the folder but doesn't find anything more so he starts about telling me the rules of the place. And my ears close down again. I look around the old room with its old curtains, dusty posters, vintage cabinets with forgotten case files all emanating fustiness. Or maybe the musty odour comes from the Warden himself, crumpled as he is in an ancient cardigan. I wonder how long he's been here. Then he wakes me to with a click of his fingers.

"People come in and out of here quickly, Sean. People like you. Kids in trouble, but also, some others. You need to stay out of trouble now. To get out of here all you need is another place to stay. A real place. I don't want you to go to prison, so keep your nose clean and that won't happen. We do things here for you. We can help. Are you listening?" He shakes his head at me like I have been in a reverie and he has been reading of some scorched tablet.

"Yes," I say. "I have nowhere." He looks at me as a dog then. He shakes his head. "You're not listening?"

"Yes! I am," I say. And then he continues to read the rules and drones on and I drift off again, but my ears do perk up when he mentions that we have to sign on or get a job during our stay. That means I'll have some money, either way, which means I'll be able to buy some socks. I have been getting by on one pair for a while. In fact, all my belongings currently fit into the sodden bag that I shouldered here. I want a place to sleep and now I don't think the Warden likes me much, but I can't speak. He eventually shows me to my room, number one. It's a bad

ANTHONY C. MURPHY

omen, as I want to keep my head down and get by. Who wants to be number one?

"Thanks."

"All right, kid. Remember, just keep your nose clean. Breakfast at eight." He hands me my key. He stares at me hard into the eyeballs. I have been in a cell for the past two days, so I don't know what he expects. He eventually breaks eye contact. I hope that's the last I see of him.

The room has a small bunk, a wardrobe, and a sink. There is a wooden chair in the corner by a window that looks out to another room across a flat asphalt roof covered in pebbledash. I take off my boots. There is a mirror above the sink that I stare into for a while, on and off, while I wash my rotten socks. I hang the socks on the hot pipes. The things in my bag I take out and put them in the wardrobe. I have a couple of books that I am halfway through, so I place them on the chair. Out of the window I see a light on in the opposite room. I wonder how many other inmates, residents... what am I called now? I decide I should go down and investigate my new surroundings, sockless.

Down the first flight of stairs and adjacent to the Warden's office is the "LOUNGE." I open the door and plunge right into a thick fog of tobacco smoke. There is a faint flicker in the far corner, which I realize is the TV. Then, through the soup, comes a real, deep, Scottish growl. "Shut the door, son!"

I do so and search for an armchair as my eyes adjust. There is silence in the room apart from the tinny chatter of the telly. *The Bill* is on and the Lounge is focused as one. I glance around and see three others beside myself. The

Walnut is here, puffing his pipe. Next to him on a big old couch is the one I take to be the voice of the growl. He's a fat man with black eyebrows. He is also puffing at a pipe. On the far side of the room and almost right in front of the box is a young lad, younger than me even, with a shaved head. He's wearing a white tracksuit. The adverts start and the lad gets up and leaves the room. Walnut rises too.

"Tea, Jock?"

"Aye."

Walnut leaves the room then, he nods at me and grins to himself. Jock turns and speaks to me.

"So! What are you in for, son?"

"Oh... Theft."

"You a burglar?"

"No. I just stole from work."

"Only we get a lot of young wee burglars in here."

"Yeah? No, I couldn't."

"What's yer name?"

"Reilly."

"I'm Jock.

"Really?"

"Aye." I see his brow furrow. "That was Bob."

I assume he means his mucker, Walnut, and not Tracksuit. He taps his tobacco pouch then.

"Do you want some? You've prob'ly nae any, eh?

"No, I'm alright."

I could actually do with a fag, but I'm not smoking some old fella's pipe, not me, no sir!

"Sure? I bet you're gaspin'. I've papers."

"Go on then. Thanks."

Jock gets out his paraphernalia and rolls me a fat smoke out of his rough shag. I watch him and wonder if he would have got on with Joe.

"There ye go!" I light it and it tastes ... exquisite. A mellowness overcomes the inside of me.

"What is that?"

Jock grins, he has no teeth, but his eyes twinkle. "It's just pipe tobacco. It's cheaper, but tasty. You need to know these things, son." He stops smiling. "When yer earning potential is limited. You know what I mean?" He wafts his hand around the general surroundings. I nod as though I've gained some knowledge. I take another drag and settle into my chair.

"So what are you here for?" I ask.

"One thing you should learn, son. Never ask anyone that question." Jock taps his nose and points at me. "Come on. I'll show you the kitchen."

Apart from Bob and Tracksuit, there is a third feller in the kitchen. He's a fat guy with long hair and a short moustache.

"Ian, this is Reilly." Jock introduces us.

"How do? What are you in for?"

Jock elbows me softly in the ribs then. "Where's this tea?" he asks no one in particular.

"Oh ... not much." I answer.

"That's right!" Ian says.

It's a big kitchen with two full benches, two stovetops, two microwaves, two massive fridges and two sinks. Twenty fellers could easily sit down to dinner together. Ian is busy making himself some kind of gourmet sandwich. Tracksuit sidles out of the room again without saying a word. The others don't seem to notice.

"Ian used to be a chef in the army," Jock says.

"So did my granddad," I say, but he's not interested.

"Here's a tip. Buy yer own food as soon as you can. This place is like school dinners," Ian says through a mouthful of bread. "Breakfast is good though. No powdered eggs."

He opens a fridge and shows me a million fresh ones and a whole pig worth of bacon and sausage, as he wiggles his eyebrows. "Do it yerself!" I don't know what to say.

Jock hands me a cup of tea. "Come on!" and we follow him back to the Lounge.

After watching some mindless TV, I feel tired. I get up and leave the Lounge, grunting a "G'night!" There are no farewells; I just go to bed. I open my door. My door. There are my socks dry on the pipes, so rigid though, I crumple them up so they soften for the morning. Looking at my boots makes me wince. I lay on the thin mattress and start to drift.

Downstairs there is a big commotion. Some residents are banging on the main door. It's five minutes past curfew, and they're causing a kerfuffle. The Warden's voice can be clearly heard telling them they're late, telling them to go away. But he must be joking, as I hear them all bundle in over the threshold, loud voices in drunken excitement, and a verbal tangle begins. I can make out the Warden's lilt as he light-heartedly admonishes someone, and Jock's bass greetings to some others. Then there are running footfalls on the stairs and past my room to another flight and upward as I fall asleep again.

There is a loud banging immediate to my head. God knows

103

what that dream was about but we are shattered. I realize it's my door. What are the rules again? What am I doing here?

"Who is it?" I ask.

"Open up! We want to talk to you." There's urgency to the voice.

"What do you want?"

"It's important." There's more than one voice, some of them laughing also. "Open the door, kid!" and the banging again. "We want to say hello." And another. "It's just us."

I guess I have to, so I do, slip out of bed, skinny in my y-fronts, and turn the latch. The door slams into me and knocks me back. I register five or six faces before the first body lifts me up and pins me against the wall.

"Where is it, you little fucker?" A weasel-faced fella spits in my face, he smells of booze.

"What?" I ask. He has a hold of my throat and with his other paw he slaps me across the cheek.

"What have you done with it? Thief!" He says this through gritted teeth and slaps me again.

Two of the other lads are busy looking under my bed and in the cupboard and out of the window. They take my bag from the chair and empty it onto the bed. They pick up my stuff, the little belongings I have, and toss them about. They laugh at my books. One lad flicks through my notebook then throws it into the sink and turns on the tap. "Don't!" I say, as if it's important. There are at least three others in the doorway, just watching and having a snicker at my plight. I haven't seen any of them before.

"I don't know what you want."

Weasel slaps me a third time as one of the searchers, a small lad with a shaved head and a beard, steps up.

"You took my stereo, man! You were here, we were all out and it's gone, man."

"I didn't," I gasp. "I just got here."

"What did you do with it?" Tiny Beard is livid. "I'm gonna caaaane someone!" He paces back and forth in front of me while Weasel holds me against the wall. I can't make any of us feel any better.

"I've been in all night," I say. "I was watching TV with Jock. Ask him."

Weasel loosens his grip and I spy an opening. Maybe 'Jock' is a magic word.

"Look if it's not in here it couldn't have been me, eh? Go and ask Jock," I say. I am shaking now. Weasel grunts and backs off and Tiny Beard rants on about caning someone as I cover my nearly naked self against the welts and the cold and the embarrassment. They shuffle out of my room and there are sighs of disappointment from a couple of the onlookers. They all go. I lock the door, go to the sink, and wash my face. I put my books on the pipes where my socks were and get back into bed. I decide to turn the light off after a few minutes and then I start to cry. I don't know why. Perhaps I'll die.

There is a banging immediate to my head. I am under no illusions, no dreams are broken this time. I had one eye open. A softer voice calls out from the other side of the wood.

"Sorry, kid!" It's the Weasel, slurring. "We were wrong."

"Go away!" I shout.

"Jock says you are all right. You owe him one."

"Go away," I say.

"He saved your arse."

"Go away," I whisper and I force myself back to sleep as the night becomes quiet.

The third time there is a carefree banging on my door, accompanied by a no-nonsense cry of "Breakfast!"

I feel like I haven't slept at all and that everything happened a minute ago. I wash my bruised face and get dressed and scrape my mop over my eyes so that I don't have to face anyone. I take my key and go downstairs.

Ian is in the kitchen frying some eggs.

"Hey!" he greets me. "Keeping busy?"

I guess everyone has heard. He takes a concerned look at my cheek.

"Don't take it personally. They just wanted someone to blame."

"But I didn't do it," I say.

"They don't give a shit about you, kidder. It's just this place, the way of things."

He flicks some fat onto the yolk, forming a cataract, and gets the edges crispy. Bubbles form and pop before he's done. He slides a couple of the monster eggs on to two slices of bread and hands me the plate. "Eat up!" he says.

I sit down at an empty bench. There's no one else here except Tracksuit; he's quietly eating a piece of toast. He avoids eye contact with me. I've never heard someone eat so quietly, and toast at that. I wonder if he knows about Tiny Beard's stereo, but I'm not about to start asking.

"Where is everyone?" I ask Ian.

"Work, most of 'em. The younguns'll be in bed still." He looks at me then. "Don't fret. You won't see that lot today. They have jobs and after that they have their other work, if you know what I mean? Besides, we had a word with them. They won't trouble you anymore."

"No?" I say. Ian makes a mime of puffing a joint, and then winks at me. I relax a little and eat a lot.

The front door and path to Trinity Road are free of any fraughtness this time in the morning. I sneak out without any conflict. The air is fresh after last night's rain and the street is clear. I have my directions and wander down the road, taking my time to soak in my surroundings. There are big urban houses everywhere. They are all set back a little but not many cars in their driveways. Not much dogshit on the pavement. I don't know what goes on here. Maybe it's all students and old people... and us. I hope I don't bump into any of those guys last night. I hear a blackbird and look up. The big beech trees are just starting to bud and then looking down I notice flowers. There are a few daffodildoes nodding in the soft verge. I chuckle to myself at that shared joke of ours and wonder how Dee is doing. Maybe if I get some money today I can call her, but then I remember my sodden notebook and everyone's addresses in it. I haven't tried to peel the pages apart yet. It's drying where my socks should be. And then I remember my priority.

I get to the job centre. It's a bureaucrat palace made of red bricks and massive plate glass windows with lots of little paper cards in place to helpfully describe the work I am underqualified for. Other men and women are gawping and are positive in jotting down case numbers with the tiny government pencils issued. I don't even peruse the employment on offer but go straight inside to the New Claims desk.

After some form filling, I emerge official. I have my social number to give to the Warden. Still, I'll have to wait a few days for a giro. And my toes curl at the prospect. And my boots sniff in resignation.

Back at the hostel I don't fancy sitting in the Lounge again just yet so I amble toward the back of the house where the pool table is. As Ian said earlier there's no one about really. One lad, a skinhead—white T-shirt, jeans and boots, is playing by himself. I'm there now so I have to face him. He is wheezing.

"All right?" he says.

"All right?" I say.

"What's with the black clothes? What are you, some kind of rocker?"

"Not really," I say.

"Well. Fancy a game?"

"Okay then."

It's a free table, the coin slots have been manacled so that the potted balls always come out. He sets them up.

"Donkey," he says.

"I don't know that one," I say. "Is it like Killer?"

"Thar's me name, you spanner!" he says.

"Oh! I'm Reilly."

"Doghouse," he says, laughing, without taking a breath; he musn't have many left. "Yer, Doghouse Reilly!" he gasps.

"Okay. Nice to meet you, Donkey," I say as he breaks. I guess I have a name, but I don't know what he's on about. And I feel bad about taking his air, even as he wheezes next to me. Maybe he's sucking mine?

He pots a few yellows and I pot a few reds. I miss a shot and he laughs at me.

"Thar's pissed on yer bonfire, innit?" His laugh is scratchy and he has to catch himself.

I don't laugh. He looks in bad shape. He is skinny and so white and cannot breathe for a minute. We stop playing and sit down. He takes out an inhaler and sucks at it.

"I've got bronchitis, don't worry. And asthma." He puffs. "What room are you in?" he asks me.

"One," I say.

"Oh, shit! I heard last night." He coughs. "I'm in room two. Sorry." He thinks. "I was asleep." He coughs again. "That was you?"

"Yeah," I say. I knew I didn't see him there. He wasn't one of the faces laughing, braying, turning me over and pawing my stuff. "It's alright." I don't blame him.

"We're all twats in 'ere though." He says. And when he gets up, he pots another yellow.

"My shot," I say.

He thinks for a second. "Nice try, smart arse!" he says, and cues another shot.

We play for a while. We are evens, but no cash. Another lad comes in and another. I think they're called Dave and Other Dave. I don't talk to them. Donkey pokes me, and gestures, as it's winner stays on, and we are both off the table, so we go outside to the garden. It's a big area with a shed and some seating. There's a pile of wood and some plastic barrels. There are birds flitting about and some feeders for cats, I am thinking, or maybe hedgehogs. The whole back garden is lined with tall, green conifer trees on three sides.

"Have you any baccy?" Donkey says.

"No. Not yet."

"Here." And he gets out a pouch of Old Holborn and rolls two thin ones with licorice paper. "Get yer lips round that," he says. "It's better outside. That lounge kills me," he says. And we take big beautiful drags and fill our young lungs with the poison of rough shag again as he splutters and coughs his tubes out. "I love it," he says. "What else is there?" And I don't know as I watch the birds. I imagine it's a hard life for some. I think he wants an answer though.

"Girls?" I say.

He looks at the floor and spits and rubs the ground with the sole of one of his calf-length, twenty-four-hole Doc Marten boots. "I guess," he says. "But they're not always around."

"No," I say. "I guess not."

"I thought I saw you once at gig."

"Yeah?"

"*Pushmastoolin'!*"

"Yeah. That was us."

"Good energy."

"Thanks. We went a different way after."

"After what?"

"After one song," I say.

It gets quiet then for a while but after the silence pops into knuckle cracking, I go back up to my room, walking through the hostel. Donkey follows. I say, "See ya!" and I open my door and notice that it's been cleaned. All my stuff is neatly piled on the bed. It doesn't take much. My notebook is on the sill, puffed up with wet words after those guys last night had drowned it. All the ink has run and nothing makes any sense. I haven't got a pen anyway. I put the journal gently into the bin and say goodbye to my shit as I hear a cough behind me at my open door.

"Come here. I'll show yer summat," Donkey says. His door is opposite mine on the landing. He opens it and I am amazed. His bedspread is a Union Jack and his window has a sheet hanging over it of the same stripes. The nationalism makes me feel queasy. He has hardback books everywhere, big, encyclopedic kind of books on history and war and the history of war. I pick one up and heft it as I peruse. And he has a record player! I put the book down.

"Jesus!" is all I can say.

"He's in there somewhere," Donkey says. "It's great innit?"

"How did you get all this stuff here?" I ask.

"My mum brought it," he says.

"Your mum! Why aren't you home?"

"Ah. She kicked me out, the daft cow. But then she felt bad. Anyway. It's just like home here. They'll let you have most things." Donkey jumps on his bed then, with his massive boots on.

"What did you do to get here anyway?" I ask.

"You should never ask that, Doghouse!" he says. "It doesn't matter. We're here now, aren't we? All of us together, punks or skins."

"I guess so," I say. I feel a sudden urge to get out of there. Those flags remind me of bad times back in Rochdale, arguing with the NF in The Fusiliers, but I play it cool and inch out of his door toward mine. "Nice room... See you later."

"Piss off then," he shouts as I shut my door.

There is a banging on my door, and I jump awake. Then there is that shout for breakfast. Whose voice is that? Fuck them anyway. I turn over. I've run out of words by this point in the book, so I try to sleep again but a key opens my door. I turn and look at an old lady with a broom and a smile. "Get up out of bed, you! Clear out!" She turns to Donkey's room and opens his door as she allows me to get decent. I see his bedspread flags all crumpled, my door wide open the whole time with nothing in it in opposition. "Right," I say, mainly to myself. "I'm sorry." And I jiggle into my jeans and throw on a T-shirt.

There's nothing to do for me but go down softly the carpeted stinking stairs and face the crowd.

I enter the lounge and sit down. There are a few fellas in here but no one that says hello. Jock grunts at me but he is distracted by the news on the TV. I sit there for an hour. I don't see Donkey or Ian. But there is a sudden influx of people. We have to sit up. The curtains are opened. The telly is turned off. There is a meeting and the chairs now get arranged into a wide horseshoe by those residents that know the drill. The Warden enters and sits. With his clipboard pressed against his cardigan, he chats to one of his assistants. A few of the younger residents amble in, sleepy-eyed, and plop onto the nearest available seats.

"Right. Let's get started! Quite a few of you are new so..." the Warden shouts, even though the room is quiet and the mood is subdued. "The rosters!" he says, holding aloft his board. "They will be up on the noticeboard outside this room every Monday. We're going to circulate the duties so you don't get stuck doing the lavs for a month.

You have to have your duty done by nine thirty ... so to speak. Then we can all move on with our lives, can't we?"

Jock raises his hand at this point.

"Yes, John?" The Warden uses his real name.

"I cannae be bending o'er behind nae jacksie, guvnor! Am an auld mon." Jock rattles his bottles of pills and tablets for emphasis. He wears a sleeveless green field jacket that has many utility pockets, each one of them a storage place for a prescription.

"Point taken." The Warden jots something down on his clipboard with a biro. "In that case, any of you too infirm to carry out your duty should come and see me in my office afterward."

There is a snort from behind me. All faces in front turn toward mine and I turn also to look. One of the young ones is asleep at the back.

"SONSHINE! OI!" the Warden bellows in his broad Brummie accent.

The young lad flicks his eyes open as we all look and snicker. As I turn back, I notice Jock has not moved; he stares straight ahead, his bushy eyebrows bunched together.

"Wakey! Wakey!" the Warden says. "What room are you?" he asks the lad at the back.

"Err... Eighteen."

"Eighteen," says the Warden and jots something down. "Right. Now then! Who is in room number one?"

Christ! My heart stops and I go bright red. It's like someone kicked me in the solar plexus. There's nothing I can do. I put my hand up.

"Right, Sean. There's been a complaint from the laundry ladies. There seems to be an awful smell. You haven't got any old food or something in there have you?"

Oh my Lord! I go even redder. The others laugh at me now. I am glad that the Weasel isn't in here. I know some of these other ones laughing were there but I can't look anyone in the eye and just stare at the floor and look at my feet. It's their fault, my feet. My socks are in my room right now. My one and only pair sitting on the radiator emanating some foul hum that I am used to, a familiar song to my nostrils, rotten cotton that I lovingly wash each night in my sink. That pungent barrier to me getting on here.

"No," I mutter.

"Well just make sure, will you?"

"Yes."

"And see me in my office after, I have letters for you," he says.

I just want him to go onto another topic, which he does—something about a daytrip to American Adventure Playland in a couple of weeks. I just hope my dole cheque comes through soon, then I can buy my feet some freshness and myself some anonymity in this place.

I am in the poolroom, playing by myself, when another young lad comes in. He's a goofy kid with acne. He looks like Corey Haim gone wrong, and he's wearing what looks to me like a blouse. He sits and watches me pot.

"Alright?" I ask.

"Just got here," he says.

"Wanna game?" I ask.

"Na!" he says.

I let the table be and go outside into the garden instead. I notice the blackbird, on his own, unflinching amid all the fucking sparrows, fighting around him. I see two blue tits and I hear a chaffinch and there are pigeons and starlings and crows and a whole world of feathers and fury in the trees and sky about me. It doesn't matter. The blackbird flits down and spikes a worm before any of us can twitch in recognition of his act.

I go back inside to see the Warden. "Sit," he says.

I don't know what's gotten into me these days, but I do what he demands.

"Sean."

"Yes."

"Your letter from the solicitor," he hands it to me, but it's already open. "You have a court date coming up." I look at it quickly, it's short and formal.

"Yes."

"You must show up to this, son. This is important."

"I know."

"It's on us here to make sure you do. Otherwise we'll have to hand you back to the police, and you can spend your time waiting in jail."

"I know," I say. His words sting but I'm getting used to it. The constant threat of incarceration is numbing to me. Where else am I supposed to go? I'm supposed to end up there is what I am thinking. I have nowhere else to go. I fall asleep with these thoughts in front of people as they talk to me.

"Listen, I know it's hard. But you can't fuck up again." The Warden looks at me to see if I'm paying any more attention. I can't help that I feel dumb in the face of authority. "We can help you here. You can always ask." I don't know what he's talking about, so I nod. "So you can take some petty cash and it will come out of your first giro.

How much would you like?" That rouses me from the stupid reverie.

"What?"

"If you need cash before the cheque comes? How much," he says.

I am amazed that someone is offering me money.

"Err... a tenner?" I know I'll probably only get sixty quid when my giro arrives. I don't want to overstretch myself.

"Sure?" the Warden says, without a blink. He takes down a tin, unlocks it, and takes out a book and a ten-pound note. He writes me down.

"This is trust, Sean. We don't steal from ourselves." He pats the tin and locks it again and puts it back on the shelf in plain view.

"Thank you," I say. "That's really... thanks."

"It's your money, Sean," he says. "But don't forget. Stop cooking your socks! Buy some new ones." And he touches his nose for effect, and his eyes twinkle. He knew all along. He was trying to save my blushes, but it didn't work. I flush at the mention of my name in any sit-down-around-a-table situation.

"I will...New socks... Money!" I say that last word out loud like an idiot discovering fire. "Thank you!"

"And don't forget your letter."

"Right," I say. I forgot. There is a letter. But it's from a solicitor, so I am just thinking, it's from a solicitor telling me what my situation is. Solicitors like to send letters.

I walk up the street and have a look at the shops. I buy three pairs of socks for one pound. All black. And that is all I buy. I am considering the greasy spoon and a bacon sarnie, but it looks like Weasel is sweeping the floor in there. It is him. All shop weary and downtrodden. He sees me as I look through the window. So that's where he spends his days. He smiles at me and waves weakly, and then he carries on sweeping. I think about how trapped he seems, but how lost he looks within that trap.

My next thought is about a pint of beer. There is a bar there on the corner called The Turks. I take my new socks and wander in to spend some more of my hard-earned money. A couple of pints is enough. It engages my brain in ways I'd forgotten in only a few days. I laugh at that and go home. Home? I laugh at that.

I sleep but a light opposite my window comes on at some point and shadows move into my room rhythmically. It's upsetting in my dreams and I don't mind the shout for breakfast.

I go down. Ian is in there frying again.

"All right, cocker?" he says. "Did you enjoy the show last night?"

I pour myself a cup of tea from the urn and squeeze into a bench. "What do you mean?" I say. Ian's moustache is resplendent in the splatter of bacon fat.

"That new lad, Bumpkin they call him. He was putting on a show at his window last night. We think you've got an admirer."

"What lad, why?" I say

"He has the window opposite you. The kid who looks like that one from that Lost Boys."

"Oh, him. What was he doing? I didn't see."

Ian does a mime of masturbating with the spatula he is holding. He laughs. "We could see from my room above yours. A few of us were playing cards but that was funny."

I don't know what to think. I get red. "Why would he do that?" I say.

"Maybe he likes you! He'll get it in the neck today," Ian says.

It, the whole it. Who gets the it? Ian seems like an old guy laughing now. I see Joe and Errol in him. But they would never give the guy the it. I spent my life not trying to get the it. And anyway...

"Okay." I don't feel like eating so I go back up to get ready for my court appearance. I haven't got a change of clothes yet so I just straighten myself up as much as I can. I flatten my hair. My feet feel warm and cozy for the first time in days though and that is something. New socks. I have some money left from the Warden's advance, so I take the bus into town.

The town court is unassuming from the outside. A squat brick building with pebble-dashed walls. I enter through some strengthened glass doors. There is a security guard inside who pats me down. I wander over to the desk for information, but the uniformed and practiced lady just points at a wall. There is a list up there with the names of all those to appear in front of the magistrates this day. I see my name, somewhere in the middle of the morning. At least I am not first, that would have made me paranoid as all hell. Then I hear my name. It shocks me.

"Hello, Sean!"

It's my mum. She's looking older, tired, but it's definitely her.

"Fuck me, Mum! What are you doing here?"

"SEAN!" She hits me on the head. "Watch your mouth."

"Get off," I say. "It's just... how did you know?"

"You have a next of kin, you know."

"What?" I can't believe that. I have no privacy. "You gave me a right shock," I say. "Come on, let's sit down." We go and find some room on a wooden bench and wait.

"So how have you been? How is the place?" Mum asks. She attempts to smooth my hair again. "You get my money?"

"I got the money, thanks!" I say. "*I squandered it on gin and cigarettes.*"

"Julie Walters?"

"Yeah," I say. "The place is okay. There's guys from all over the place. Scousers, Brummies, Geordies, Jocks."

"God. We must live in the crime capital of Britain. There can't be anything left to steal, is there?"

"They're not all fuckin' thieves, Mum!"

"Language, Sean! You're spending too much time with them already. It's rubbing off." I laugh at that.

"I don't have much fucking choice," I say. She taps me on the head again. "Sorry!" I say.

"Ssssh! Will you?" she says. "What have they all done then, if they're not thieves?"

"I dunno... Something, I guess." I start talking in urgent whispers. She's made me aware of others' eavesdropping, those others waiting here, hungry for gossip and scandal in the courthouse. We straighten ourselves on the bench.

"*Something* is right. And what about you? I thought I taught you the difference between right and wrong." She's whispering too now. I think she is about to lick a tissue and apply it to me.

"Yeah...I just. I didn't... I was stuck," I say, and shrink

away from her. "Don't Mum!"

"That's weak," she says, putting away her hanky.

"Well you didn't want to help," I say. She takes a gulp of air.

"There's no way I was paying for *his* funeral. Not after what he did," she says.

"I guess not," I say. I remember what he did. I remember her bruises, and her going out with sunglasses on, in Rochdale. No one wears sunglasses in Rochdale. Not only because it's always cloudy, but because it looks like you're a poser if you do. There's nothing worse in that town, on our street, than being called a poser. I also remember Joe had said that wasn't all there was to it though, the black eye.

"What did he do?" I ask.

"He never told you? When he came back? When you were all pally and working together?" she huffs.

"No." I don't let on that he told me he wasn't the only one to blame.

"Well, you were too young," she says.

"Are you only allowed to cry once?"

"No."

"I wasn't that young," I say.

"I was," she says. "Too young to get trapped like some ..." She twitches, her hands shake, but she catches herself and stops. "Anyway, it doesn't matter now that he's dead."

May the void never be so succinct with me, I think. But I don't voice it. I am an ignoramus. I shouldn't want to know. I shouldn't, but I do.

"Maybe it matters to me, Mum," I say. "What did he do?"

She looks me in the eye then. She has green eyes and

they are youthful, full of light. I see myself in them. They are so familiar to me I would never have to see them again, yet I would know them in my sleep. And they smile at me. I would say they are full of love, but I know better than to believe such things. I have seen them go just as glittery with meanness as Joe's eyes used to whenever, well whenever they wanted to, but usually when I had been acting selfishly. I can see in her eyes that I am a disappointment, she rolls them and they cloud and change, unlike the weather here, quickly, without warning. They are even tearing up a little.

"Okay, Seany. If I tell you, some of it, will you drop it? I don't want to think about any of it anymore." She says.

"Okay," I say.

"Okay," she says. And she sits up and takes a breath and fiddles with her handbag. "Okay," she says again, "we'd been at The Entwistle, drinking with Vinny and Sheila, singing those old Irish songs up on our feet. You were staying over at your mate's house. Do you still see Dickie?"

"No," I say. "Not much chance anyway, living where I do."

"No," she says. "I guess not. He doesn't visit?"

"Why would he?" I ask. "Go on."

"Yeah. So, it was the usual at The Entwistle Arms, but I could see Joe, your dad, was flirting, and god knows, I was at the end of my tether with that. With all of it. The animals he used to bring home. The pub every day. The betting on the horses. He spent more time at the bookies than he did at home and more time in the pub than either. At least he'd had a decent job before. When that place shut down, and he had to get temporary work, it started getting worse. It was like he didn't care anymore. Not that he ever did, I don't think, not really. We had fun sometimes. And he enjoyed you until you turned two years old and became a single-minded whirlwind. There were times though." She stopped. I wanted to hear about those times. I thought I could remember good times. Maybe one day I would. I had snatches of memory that had laughter in them. And not just that hard braying sarcastic laughter.

"Go on," I say.

"There was one time," Mum says, and she starts to cry, here in the courthouse waiting room, "when you came into our room, because you, Sean, had heard something, you must have been about three, and we were having sex, you know, sorry! But he, Joe, your dad, was so angry at the interruption. You were just saying 'Mum'. We must have woke you... He got up and hit you so hard that you flew off your feet." She had to breathe. "I should have done something then... I left it for years... but I always remembered the look on your face, not angry, just so... disappointed or something... you got up and walked away to your bedroom." She had to breathe again. "You changed from a baby that night. You never wanted to come into our bed after that."

"Was that it?"

"He didn't do it again. Is that what you mean?"

"How about you?"

"Well, I'll tell you," she says, shaking a bit, "he had a temper."

"Have you got any smokes, Mum?" I ask. I can't make her feel any better. She wipes her face with a tissue from her handbag.

"Only menthol," she says. I have to think about now.

So we go outside again. I tear the filter off the cigarette and light it on the steps, and I smoke like it's my last dramatic fag. "What are you doing?" she starts to ask. There are many people out here, arguing, most of them. I see a big skinhead, and he sees me. I hope it's his third act and he gets sent down but I don't even know his first act. I see the difference between guys in suits placating these other guys out here, and some, but not many, girls they represent, those looking out of place in buttoned up shirts with tattoos peeking out, who have nothing much else but loud voices about how unlucky they are and, "*Do something about it!*" shouts. The whole thing makes me sick. This is all a joke I have become a part of. I look at the pub opposite, but I don't want to go there.

"What did your solicitor say about all of this, Sean?" Mum asks.

"Nothing," I say. "He's not even here yet."

"Let's go back in," she says.

She puts her arm around me, and when we are back through security down on a wooden bench, waiting, I ask again, "Was that it though?" and we start whispering again.

"No," she says. "I knew what he was like." She gets another hanky out.

"What do you mean?" I say.

"That night, after years of this and that and the other something happened in my head. We'd been together too long all of us. When I saw him flirting and with all those others, some of them he knew, he knew more than he let on he knew. And he'd played all his money again. And cursed about my cooking soapy potatoes one too many times... I just told him to get out," Mum says.

"Why then, though?" I ask.

"Well," she sobs a bit, "it's because I thought you were old enough as well."

"Oh!" is all I say.

"I didn't say it to him. I just said that I'd had it. It was over."

"And he hit you then?"

"Yes," Mum says. "He was mad. But I didn't care. I had a way out. I'd already been seeing Steve."

"Oh, *him*," I say. "I see." She won't look me in the eye either now.

"Yes," she weeps a liitle more, "and all the neighbours wanting a butty and a natter. To be good neighbours. But that wasn't it. They wanted the juicy gossip. I wasn't hungry for their talk! The last thing I want is a butty and a natter with Sheila, who your dad was probably... you know... "

"Shagging?" I ask.

"Yes. Shagging. Thank you. I don't know why Vinny ever even tried pulling him out of the canal," she says, "all of us at it."

"It didn't make any difference, in the end," I say and I put an arm around her.

"No. No. I guess not," she sobs. "Good riddance!" Mum says. "Are you angry?" she asks.

"Well," I say. "Maybe. Not really. I knew already, I think." And then my name is called by the court officer, so I have to appear up front through the wooden door. I give my mum a kiss, I get her to sit, and I walk in, shakily, to face the metronome.

It is my second time in court. What kind of animal are they, magistrates? On a supposedly superior strata, for no pay at that, just for the duty of being lofty? Three upright citizens seated so high above scruffy little me, judging. They do not make eye contact though. Power does that both ways. They all peruse their notes as if they know by looking at official scribbles that they can determine a person. They're like some kind of nontactile phrenologist. They haven't got a clue. They are told what to do by those in the middle of us, those who have read a little and decided to be safe, the ones wearing neckties. All I hear is blah, blah. Then they ask me to recognize my name so I perk up but all I am required to say is "Yes." I came all this way for that.

"Nothing happened, Mum." I grab her hand and walk out of the building. "Come on. Let's go and get a drink," I say.

"No. Wait. I don't want one," she says.

"A cup of tea?"

"Oh. Right. Sure," she says. So we go. "What happened?"

"Nothing."

We get to the greasy spoon and jam ourselves into a corner table. The place is packed, being so close to the courthouse. It's full of mean looking buggers smoking their heads off. Everyone looks like a mean bugger to me these days. We get a strong mug of tea each. Mum doesn't take milk anymore, I notice.

"I have to come back. They set the date for three weeks."

"Why?" she asks. "I thought it'd be done with today."

"I was hoping," I say, "The prosecution weren't ready. I'm still at the mercy of the court and in the custody of the probation service."

"Oh, Seany! I'm sorry."

"Well. I don't think I'm ready, never mind them. What if they send me down?"

"Well what did Mr. Lillicrap say?"

"Who?"

"Your solicitor. You know he looks like that TV presenter," she says. "Curly hair, buggy eyes." She laughs and searches for a connection in my eyes.

"Yeah, I guess he does," I say. "He said, First Offence. I'll just get a fine." I remember.

"There you go then." She takes a sip and smiles and looks away. There is a commotion at the door: some lanky lad with mad eyes is cursing his sweetheart and she, the sweetheart, spits back at him from her seat, make-up running down her cheeks and spittle running down his, both of their faces clenched and who would ever know if they ever loved each other but I think it's a guy that I worked with Barry, and his girlfriend Janice, locked in some ever loving embrace.

"But still," I say, "what do I even do when they release me?"

"You have a bit of time, eh?" she says.

"You know. You could write to the court and say I'll come and stay with you, that I'll be in your custody," I say.

She splutters. "No. Not again... I'm not being responsible. You're eighteen now. Besides, I don't want you messing up and it be on me. And we have no room. *He* wouldn't like it anyway."

"I guess not," I say. *He*, again, the new him. I don't want to be a part of that. "It's too far away anyway," I say.

"I'm sorry Seany, but you've got to handle this

yourself."

There is a tidal wave in every sip of tea.

"Let me know how you get on. I won't make it up to court the next time. I can't take another day off work," she says. "Here," she gives me ten pounds.

"Sure," I say.

She kisses me goodbye and I wander off to get my bus back to the hostel.

"He's back!" Ian shouts, and ruffles my hair as I enter the kitchen. There is a smell so like a Tuesday night. What does a Tuesday night smell like? Jock is in there, and the Walnut. And Bumpkin sits quietly in a corner by himself.

"You must be very long winded," Ian says to me.

"What do you mean?" I say.

"They couldn't finish your sentence for you?" There is no laughter, except for a deep gurgling from the pit of Jock, so maybe someone found it funny. "Good one, Ian," Jock says.

"What you making, Ian?" I ask. He's busy at the pans again.

"Tripe 'n' onions," he says.

That explains it. We had some routines during the week at our house regarding meals for tea. By Tuesday the roast was all gone, and Dad liked to bring some piece of offal back from the market. He'd usually wait until Tuesday anyway because nothing got caught or slaughtered at the weekend, or if it did it got stuck at the abattoir.

"You want some?"

"Sure," I say and sit down. "Saves me going to the chippy."

"Good lad. No one else does." There is another deep gurgle from Jock, and he unzips a pocket and rattles himself out a dosage of something or other. He gulps the pills down with help from his mug of tea and gasps afterward. I look at him. His heavy eyebrows so low that I can't see his eyes, his big chest is slow in raising after the deepest of breaths.

"You okay, Jock?" I ask.

"Aye lad, nae bother," he says. "Get us another drop of tea, would you?"

"What did your last slave die of, Jock?" Ian pipes up.

"Bloomin' cheek," Jock says. I get up and siphon out the swill from the monster tea kettle into two mugs.

"I think it's done, Ian," I say.

"Sit down, you incompetent. I'll do it," Ian says, as he goes about filling it up again. "So. You had no good news today then?" he asks me. I look about the room at who is listening. Jock has his eyes closed and is still breathing heavily. Walnut is puffing away at his pipe. I notice then that Bumpkin has sidled out. I don't blame him, but it looks suspicious. I wonder if they have confronted him with his high-visibility wanking yet. I don't want to ask. I have no secrets.

"No. Nothing happened," I say.

"You'll be here for a bit then?" Ian asks.

"Looks like it," I say.

"Good," he says, and sets before me a plate of gelatinous white mess swimming in milk, smothered in onions, peppered with pepper and smelling like Tuesday. "Eat up!" he starts to say, but I beat him to it. I am hungry no more that night.

"Footy game today! Any of you lads got your own boots?" the Warden asks. He has cornered us all in the kitchen. There are some murmured answers of yes, but I haven't committed, yet I want to play. We can't help ourselves. It's a calling. "Well there's some kit. Have a look in the laundry. We have a bus coming after breakfast. This game is for you lads. And you kids had better be good. But it's just for fun. But you'd better win. For fun's sake." The Warden laughs to himself and goes back to the office and some of the young ones run into the other room to look at the kit. I follow slowly and manage to find an old pair of boots and shin pads.

"You won't need those, lad!" Tiny Beard laughs. "You won't get near the ball." He pushes by and bumps me, and I wonder if we are on the same team today.

Another lad, Zim, a small guy with muscles, says, "Ouch!" and laughs too. I am left in there by myself, I think, so I root around for some shorts, as I can't play in my tight jeans, my only pair at that. I find an old rugby shirt, New Zealand, All Black; I like it.

"Suits you," Donkey says as he finds me there. He tries on a pair of old goalie gloves. "You play much?" he asks.

"Yeah," I say. "Not for a while."

"Where?"

"Middle. Central. In the middle."

"I get you, man!" Donkey laughs. "Well, just pass to the little beardy cunt up front and don't worry about it. He'll love it."

"Who are we playing?" I ask.

"Just some other guys like us. Another hostel. It'll probably be only six- or seven-a-side. Last time only ten showed up and there were some really old guys. They've gone. Old guys out, new guys in. It's the way of this place. They keep you moving. It depends on who has a court appearance."

"What about you?"

"Oh, I'm here for a while. Complications!" Donkey says. I nod and wonder how I can make it all go faster.

The bus turns up, so we get on. It is half full of guys all sitting in the back rows. Guys like us that I don't know.

"Lurch!" Donkey shouts a welcome to a big, shaven-headed guy sitting in the back corner, over the wheel. Lurch gives a toothy grin and welcomes Donkey with a deep, happy growl. He looks big sitting down even. I plonk down then by a window in the middle as the rest of our hostel 'team' climbs aboard. They all ignore me, two by two, but I don't care. We drive away after a headcount by Emily with her clipboard.

We drive to a park that has a couple of flat fields with goalposts already in place. There is no netting though. The lads get off the bus and the chat never subsides, even though we separate into our loose looking teams—we know who we are. We take our positions and the game is afoot.

Kick off, and I go up for a header with Lurch, his elbow jabs into my ribs, on purpose. I fall, but the game goes on around me. I gasp as I get to my feet and watch as they score from the first defense-splitting pass. I shake my head. They are playing that game. Donkey and Tiny Beard yell something at me from different ends of the pitch but I can't hear them or comprehend and I don't even care. I know what to do. The game goes on around me. I gasp. We can't rely on the lads at the back who don't seem to know how to read a pass. Our team is yelling things at everyone, as if they know, but I can't hear anything that makes sense. I know to lay off and make Lurch seem ridiculous with his challenges. The game goes on around me, I gasp. Lurch thinks that he has me covered, but he doesn't. I stay away from him and let him make mistakes. He gives the ball away easily and I mop it up. I find the spaces where Tiny Beard is and feed it toward him. He scores. He is confident. It feels easy after a while. We are as crap as each other with our bad passing. Donkey starts giving the ball straight to me after a while, the other lads become superfluous, they are kids pretending to know how to kick a ball. I feint, remember to keep my head up, take one more breath than the others. The game becomes a blur but within that there are moments of clarity, when a perfect cross can lead to a goal. I can breath, but I gasp. It's the scorer who runs around like an idiot. I don't do anything other than move and pass. It is good to run and also feel my feet connect in a powerful way again with a leather sphere. Sometimes I want to just smack it as far as I can, as high as I can. But I don't. This is a mess, but it's not a practice. I don't have the time for that. I wonder if I ever will again. Those days when we just kicked a ball to each other in a fallow field, when my ribs didn't hurt and I could curl corners. When we were free to make mistakes and yet still have to go and get the ball from wherever it had landed because we were the ones who needed that ball to carry on making our mistakes. I pass and move. I don't do anything that is winning. It doesn't matter. I don't even care. It just becomes a game of movement or not. We are as fluid as our breathing allows. Stop. Someone puts the ball in the nonexistent net again to end it.

Afterward it's just sweat and we sit on the bus as if none of it ever happened and I already forget the intricacies of who did what. Tiny Beard sits at the back and lords it up like he's won the World Cup. Lurch pats me on the head as he walks by me and says, "Good game, kid!" I take a deep breath and my ribs tickle my lungs, or the other way around. I feel bruises coming on.

The trip to American Adventure Playland had been organized weeks ago, before I even got to the bail hostel. And it was a compulsory trip for those of us without a 'real' job, regular job or a heart defect. A 'real' job meant that you didn't need a regular job. A heart defect meant that you didn't give a shit. I didn't know this at the time. Guys with heart defects had 'real' jobs but couldn't get regular jobs. Guys with regular jobs could get 'real' jobs if the 'real' guys would let you but not the other way around. You could only get a heart defect if you had a regular 'real' job for ages. I don't know. So I went on the trip.

Funds were in place and the staff had been allocated to be with us. I think they all had a vote on it when the average age of the people in the room was seventeen. It must have seemed like a good idea at the time.

After breakfast, and after I had cleaned the first-floor toilet, a minibus pulls up outside. Ten of us pile into it. Donkey wheezes on board, and Tiny Beard, Tracksuit, and some other young faces I had seen in the lounge but not spoken to yet. Bumpkin gets on and sits near the driver.

A kid they call Tritch sits next to me. He's one of Jock's 'wee burglars,' and a good one apparently, according to himself. Jock is always on the lookout for lads that can shimmy up a drainpipe and do break-ins. The sexual connotations of that have us laughing sometimes behind Jock's back, never to his face though. Jock has the face of Ben Nevis.

"This is gonna be boss!" Tritch says.

"Yeah," I say.

"You ever been on Monster Canyon?"

"No."

"What about The Rattlesnake?"

"No," I say, "it was more about the Rickety Mouse and the Log Flume when I went."

"Kid's stuff," he laughs. I had been to this crazy playground once before with a sister of my mum's, my Aunt Kay. It was nice of her, but I'm not one for the plastic thrills of rollercoasters or the endless queues to get to that empty feeling. I don't know how to say that to Tritch, who seems so thrilled already. He starts to spark up.

"Don't do that," I say.

"We can smoke."

"Not that, you can't. She's getting on." I point to the Warden's assistant, Amy, as she boards the bus with her clipboard. "Or go and sit at the back, maybe?" I say.

"Good spot, nice one, man!" Tritch says, and he pockets the half spliff he was waving about. But he stays where he is. "So what are you here for man?" he asks me. I just deflect the question and nod in her direction as she seems like she's going to speak.

Amy counts some heads. "Okay lads," she says. "What's going to happen is this..." and she gives us a monologue about not breaking rules that has an undermurmur of teenage ignorance from the back of the vehicle as the wheels start to move. I try to cover my head and get extra sleep but all I can smell is toilet bleach.

As soon as we get through the gate all the lads split up and run to their prime destinations—the big rides. There are some other even younger ones here in crocodile formation with teachers. It's a Tuesday in April, so the place is only half full. It's a place of granite, fiberglass, and metal, all gaudily painted. There is a fake feeling to everything and a stench of burning meat and burnt plastic cheese. There are isolated bursts of screamed excitement like a sugar rush or drunkenness.

I see Bumpkin at a queue for a slow, high ride. He's wearing the same flowery blouse. "This one has good views of everything," he says, as I try to slip by. I stop.

"Oh. Is it a good one?" I ask him.

"I dunno."

"Well let me know," I say and wander off.

Tritch is on another ride. "Come on, man, you've got to try this one. I've just been on twice! There's no little ones allowed on. It's boss, man!"

We strap into a seat together in a bucket on a train track. The bucket starts off jerkily backward; it rises to an incredibly high point. I look out to the fields beyond. Trees like moss, fields of sheep like cotton buds, towns like blocks on a map. We trundle for a few seconds and then start to hurtle down forward toward a vertical loop, but the brakes come on almost immediately. Something does not feel right and Tritch suddenly shouts, "This didn't happen last time!" We get to the point at the top of the loop and stop, upside down. We hang in our belts for half a second, as my hair leaves my scalp. "Shit!" I gasp and grip the restraining bar. Then we go backward, jerking with the brakes. The bucket car takes us to the top point, very slowly again. We stop there and we wait. I don't regard the view this time. I am looking at the track that runs away below us.

"Shit, man! We're stuck," Tritch says.

"Third time lucky," I say.

"Shut up! ... Should we get out?"

"You can if you want," I say. I don't expect him to, but he unbuckles and then manages to squeeze out from under the restraining bar. "What are you doing? I didn't mean it... look there's someone coming." There are some little dot-sized men down there, maybe they are walking to us.

"You wait up here. I'm off," Tritch says. He climbs from the car, onto the track and grabs a hold of the near vertical scaffold. He clambers down effortlessly to the part of the track where it is less vertiginous and starts to walk down. The dots down there start waving at him, he's far enough away from me now that the only sound I can hear is the wind up here. I wait and I watch Tritch as he waves at them also. Their waving gets a bit more frantic though, and I feel the car start to budge. I jerk forward and stop and jerk forward and stop. They are obviously trying to get the thing down slowly, a bit at a time. Tritch walks on, he can feel the rumble on the track far ahead I reckon, as he suddenly jumps to one side and looks back at me. I can't see his eyes yet but I am closer. The men down below are still waving him off, but he's not looking at them. He leaves the track as he sees my car getting nearer in its staccato approach. I am getting properly jiggered about. Tritch is now off the track and dangling from the side of the ride, holding the scaffold, finding a foothold. Then they let the brakes off fully and I hurtle down the track toward the men at the bottom and past Tritch, who gives me a big grin as our faces meet for a blip. It makes me laugh seeing him like that. The brakes squeal on as I near the end of the descent; white sparks fly and I close my eyes. This time they manage to stop the thing before it goes on into the loop. I am thrown back in my seat with a whiplash. Three men in boiler suits are in attendance when I open my eyes again.

"Are you all right, kid?"

"What a thrill!" I say and clamber out. I look up to see Tritch walking down the track toward us.

"That bloke's a nutter!" one of the guys says.

I wait for him, but he decides to leap over the railings before he gets to us, and he wanders away into the depths of the park instead of facing these fellers. The three of them turn their attention to the car then and I am left standing there. There is no apology. I feel lucky enough to sense the concrete beneath my thin-soled Chelsea boots once more. There is not even a suggestion box around. I amble off then... to find a saloon.

The bar of The Dry Gulch has an exterior mocked up to look like some Wild West cantina but the Americana doesn't stop at 1890. Inside it is a blinking kaleidoscope. Every corner is a Silicon Valley trip—from pinball to Pac-Man. There is a jukebox, too, a big old Wurlitzer, playing Elvis, playing Elvis, playing Elvis.

"Pint of Guinness," I say

"Are you with your parents?" the barman asks me.

"How old are you?" I say.

"None of your business," he says. "ID?"

He's got a big nose for a small fella and a stupid haircut, I don't know where he gets his confidence from, wearing that crazy outfit too, and a massive sheriff badge with the name Lionel. I have no identification on me though. We all had to leave that at the hostel. So, I am at his mercy. I know he will never serve me. We stare at each other for a second longer than I was hanging upside down before, just so that I can give him my thoughts, through his eyeballs, about how victimized I feel by this situation. I have to walk away. It's a big old room though, there are punters by the score. I spy a couple of half-drunk pints of lager on a table and grab one as I walk by and take a big mouthful of it as I walk out. It tastes like the death of beer. I put the glass down on a table by the door as I leave, but I hear a shout behind me, a proper upset, "Oi! That's my pint!" so I start to run.

I get on the bus at two thirty with a nose swollen and a bloody hanky. The driver gives me no notice as he is reading the paper and sipping from his flask. Bumpkin is asleep, apparently, on a seat next to the driver. There is no one else onboard yet. I go to the back, where the toilet is, and have a look at myself in the mirror.

Christ, I am mess. The beer wasn't worth it. I swab myself with more toilet roll. There is a welt above my right eye that will become something but at least the bleeding has stopped. I take some more paper and go and find a seat in the middle of the bus. The others start to pile on, full of talk about their own adventures. Tritch finds me and sits down. He smells happy.

"That was boss, man!" he says.

"Yeah," I say.

"What happened to you?"

"I walked into a lamppost," I say.

"Idiot," he tuts, as he puts in his Walkman. I curl up into myself as we drive home.

I wake up with the *Breakfast!* herald ringing through my dream. My nose is sore and I dare not trumpet. I get dressed gingerly as I ache in unexpected places. I have not had to run for a while, since I left school probably, and my calf muscles twinge. I don't understand joggers. I have done enough cross-country to last me into old age. I take a look in the mirror, but I don't want an argument so I untie my boots from outside the window where they air at night. They are heavy, and I notice that they are full of little rocks, the pebbles from the flat roof between our windows. I look over but Bumpkin has his curtains closed. "The little git. What is he playing at?" I say to the mirror. I climb onto the sill and empty the rocks back out of the window. "Is it some kind of signal?" I wonder at myself. "Or is he just showing off his burglary skill?" I would be angry but it's such a bizarre and harmless thing. I go down to breakfast to baffle it out.

"Doghouse!" Donkey greets me. He wheezes and spits into a hanky.

"Donkey!" I say. "And it's Sean."

"Alright, kidder? How was the trip? Woah! What happened to your face?" Ian asks. He is whisking some eggs up in a large stainless steel bowl and the sound grates and has me clenching my jaw.

"He walked into a lamppost!" Tritch laughs. They all do. Tracksuit is in the corner; he isn't laughing. Bumpkin isn't in here. There are a couple of others I don't recognize yet. One lad with a perry haircut and a lad with his back to me.

"Hello, Ian," I say and grab myself a mug of tea before moving on to the poolroom.

Bumpkin is in here, playing by himself again, practicing trick shots.

"Hoi!" I get his attention. "What was all that about?" I put my mug down and walk up to him. He straightens up to answer me. I stand right in front of him then and he fronts me off. He is smaller than me and has bad posture, his hair is a greasy mop, but then so is mine.

"What do you want?" he asks.

"What the fuck did you do that for?"

"Do what?" He is shaking a little at the confrontation and I feel bad already.

"Put all those stones in my boots? Don't deny it. It must have been you."

"Oh, that. I forgot. They were your boots?"

"Of course they were. It's my room."

"I didn't know. I was only messing about."

"Whose boots did you think they were then?"

"I don't care. Shouldn't leave things lying about."

"I was giving them some fresh air."

"You got athlete's foot?" he asks. Not anymore I think. And the tension vanishes.

"Just cut it out, will you?" I say.

"Don't tell me what to do," he mutters.

"I'm not. I'm telling you what not to do."

A couple of the others come in then. Maybe they heard something, but I am not that bothered.

"What's going on?" Donkey asks, walking over, his

eyes dart from me to Bumpkin and back. He sniffs the air like a mole searching for a morsel of anything.

"Nowt," I say.

"Nuthin'," says Bumpkin.

"Right... Game of killer?"

"Sure."

Midway through the game, only me and Donkey are left on to pot, and I am about to take a shot. There is a yellow lined up and I strike the cue ball. Bumpkin is standing by the side of the table. He puts his hand out and grabs the yellow, takes it off, and then rolls it back toward me as the white goes in a pocket. It's a stupid thing to do but I don't question it. I don't even see anything except what I am going to do to him. I throw my cue on the ground and grab a cube of blue chalk and throw it in any direction. There is a fog that comes down and clouds everything else, even the room; it is just me and Bumpkin as I rush around to grab his stupid flowery shirt in my fist and pull him toward myself. I see a sick little grin on his face turn into a snivel and I feel him shake beneath my paw. I shove him away from me then onto the ground. I am aware that I am shouting something at him. Something. "You fucking little prick!" The room goes quiet after the echo though. There is a hush of expectancy. Or there was never any sound. Bumpkin is in my tunnel vision. He's a crumpled heap and he puts his arms up around his head. The other lads are all standing now behind me, waiting. I can feel them as one on my shoulder, not even whispering, just grinning and watching with wide open eyes. There is a demon on my shoulder willing me to kick. There is a demon in my eyes willing me to tear this shaking doll's head from his shoulders. But I don't. My rage dissipates, I can't keep it up. It leaves me as quickly as it came. I start to hear the normal frequency of the room and I can see the peripheries again. I know where I am. Bumpkin stays on the ground but I turn to walk away. There are groans of disappointment from around as I leave. Donkey calls after me, "That's two quid you owe me!"

"I don't give a fuck!" I shout back, and I head off up to my room. The room has been stripped. I have no sheets on my bed again. I go to the toilet and sit down, shit and cry.

I am watching *The Bill* in the lounge. Jock and Walnut are puffing away near me. Their heaving lets out and something other than just smoke drifts into the air and dances in the low evening sunlight that rays through gaps in the leaden curtains.

"They should just lock the bugger up," says Walnut about some character on the telly.

"Aye," says Jock.

I feel tired so I get up to go my bed.

"Sit down, Sean," Jock says. Walnut gets up instead then and opens the door. Light floods the room and frightens the ethereal cobwebs. I look at the back of Walnut as he checks the hallway. "Go get Ian," Jock says to him. Walnut closes the lounge door leaving me and Jock in the late smoky gloom again. It's spooky but I know to bite my tongue. There is silence and I have nowt to do but stare at images and try to act cool. The adverts are on and I am seriously considering buying a Ford Escort, until my reverie gets punctured by the door bursting open and then Ian slaps me on the head. "All right, cocker?" he says.

"What's going on?" I say. I don't get up. Walnut shuts

the door on us again and stays out. The pair of them have me surrounded with their bulk.

"We have a favour to ask," Ian says. I look at Jock but he is intent on the telly.

"What?" I say.

"Listen," Jock says. "We need you to do a job for us." He doesn't look at me and I can't make out his deep-set eyes.

"Yeah?" I don't know what to say or do for the best.

"You owe me," Jock says.

"He's right," Ian says. "We've made it easy for you here."

I look at them both and feel the sweat and heat between us. I want to leave. I want to escape, but I sit still and do as I am told.

"Okay. Doing what?" I ask.

"You just have to be in a place and pick up a package and bring it back here," Ian says.

"I would do it, laddie, if I was you, but I cannae. It would help us out. I would do it if I was you."

There is silence then, the screen even goes blank for half a second. The dark takes over but I can still hear Jock's rattling breath and Ian's squirming fat arse in the chair next to me. The screen comes alive again with part two of tonight's episode.

"What about court though?" I say. "I have to... I have to keep my nose clean." I don't know how to say anything other than that. I don't want to go to jail for these cunts. Jock gets out an inhaler and puffs in shallow way, the wheeze of which is louder than a siren.

"Dinnae fash yerself. You'll be alright. No one will know anythin'".

"You do owe us, Sean," Ian says resting a fat hand on my shoulder. I feel the weight of him.

"Okay. I'll help you out."

"Good lad. Come with me and we'll go over it," Ian says. So I go to his room to finesse tomorrow's activities.

I wait on the street corner next to the Cathedral. I have ten minutes before this guy Pete shows up. I go into the pub opposite, The Cathedral's Arms, to get a quick half. They aren't ready and open yet though. Sorry! They turn me away so I go inside the real church.

There is some kind of choral practice going on. I sit at the back, on a pew. I haven't been to church for a while, apart from Joe's original cremation. This is one that is not my stripe anyway but it's not that different, just bigger, more impressive, more peaceful. The voices spiral in this place, become some overwhelming shell of an echo chamber. I can hear each part, each pitch from the flat to the sharp to the deep rumbling of some joyful-voiced, grizzled old man standing at the back.

There is beauty to the phrases, all of them together. I am rooted yet the roof is so high I feel like I am upside down in Noah's Ark with my feet in the air. I don't get what they are on about, and they don't all look happy, some serious and some so sure enough in their fear that it makes me laugh when I see their faces and yet I feel it is something else. I close my eyes instead and soar away with them all for five minutes of ...

I remember being an altar boy and I remember being in church with Joe—his duty to god, to make me a Catholic—because it had been done to him.

I think about Joe, how he had never cared about money

that much, and what he would think about me now, doing this. Not only did I steal from work, I am sitting in a fecking church and about to do something similar.

He had taken me to ancient stone circles and shown me faded frescoes in Saxon naves. We were better than this, he'd said, about church, as we stood in the crumble of Lindisfarne. He apologized, but laughed, because he had gone through it too, the altar boy thing. We were better than priests, he said, who were just other con men, no better than thieves. We were better than thieves, better than everyone on our street. We were better than the toe rags and the hitman. There was only one hitman, Tony. We were better than the drug dealers and glue sniffers, obviously you have to start small. We were better than everyone, Joe said, but no better than Vincent who lives next door. Remember that, he said.

This thought opens my eyes as it reminds me that I have a guy to meet. I exit the church before any crescendo comes crashing, before I feel any epiphany. I do feel a little bit loopy though, like coming out from the cinema in the afternoon. It shouldn't still be daylight. But it is.

The plan is that he, Pete, my man to meet, has a bag, a plastic Tesco bag. I see a man with a bag, I assume it's the man, Pete. He's wearing all blue denim, and has a feathery haircut, like a fan of Status Quo.

"Pete?" I ask him as he stands there. The man with the bag looks me up and down.

"What the fuck do you want, kid?" he says.

"The bag?" I say. He tucks it under his arm suddenly.

"Fuck off, kid. What are you some kind of psycho? Kids these days. Go mug an old granny instead."

"What?" I say

"You heard."

"You are Pete," I say.

"So what? Lucky guess, every other bugger's called Pete."

"Not where I'm from, it's Dave, every other bugger is Dave," I say. The man with the plastic bag, who I am sure is Pete, a part of the plan, laughs then.

"Fuck off," he says though. "I'm meeting someone."

"Yeah, me!" I say.

"Nah!" Pete says. His eyes flick about, trying to find some focus that he doesn't quite get. "They wouldn't send a skinny little punk."

"Jock had no choice," I say. I can see his whole attitude change at the name.

"Jock didn't tell me," Pete says, but he loosens a bit and lets the bag down from the cozy solitude of his armpit. He looks relieved.

"Ian says they can't use the phone in the hostel anymore. It's short notice," I say.

"Right." Pete's eyes shift about. He doesn't want to let go but he has no choice. "Don't fuck me over kid," he says and thrusts the bag at me as he walks off down the street, flicking his hair and turning his collar up.

"Dick," I say quietly. I hold the bag and I look in it. There is a package all wrapped up. I daren't take it out. It's kind of heavy. I stick my head in, but it doesn't smell. I sniff, look around and head back to my bus stop.

"What time's the next number forty-two?" I ask an old granny next to me.

"Half an hour," she says. I notice a bookshop down the street a little, so I go in there.

It's a grot hole, still their books are all new; it's not a secondhand charity shop. I riffle through the literary section to the D's. They have some J. P. Donleavy and I see The Onion Eaters, I grab it, as I haven't seen a copy for ages. I read over the back of it. "This is your dad's ever favourite book. He loved it!" "It tickled me! Joe Reilly." It speaks to me, the book. I know that I am going a little mad, but I don't really care. I see the price and then I empty my pockets. I have three pounds and I need to get another bus ticket. I look up at the ceiling and the walls but I see no cameras so I put the book in the bag. I do it quick, matter of fact like, but I feel a surge of adrenaline, an urge to fart that I hold in, an urge to run that I stall, and my hand shakes a little as I move down the aisle slowly, acting all cool, as if nothing out of the ordinary has happened, and it hasn't really. But ...

"Put the book back," she says.

"Jesus!" I jump, a shock hits me like a jarred funny bone and then the shock shoots up to my armpits, which prickle intensely. Meanwhile my stomach gives in to some rumble and I do let out a little squeak. My face gets hot. Then I turn to see who she is. It's Mary, from school, all dressed in black with black hair tied back. She is smiling, nearly laughing and her eyes are green. She reminds me of our old cat, Tara, in a funny way, although that cat was grumpy all the time. It calms me a little, the sight of her.

"Hello, Sean," she says.

"Hi, Mary. It is you. You scared me..." She laughs. "You've dyed your hair. I was going to buy it... I just... I was... I haven't finished looking... you know?" I say.

"Sure. Sure. What is it anyway?" I fish the book out

and she takes it from me. "Donleavy? I haven't heard of him."

"He was one of my dad's favourites," I say as she moves closer to me. The fresh smell of her reminding me of better times when I wasn't surrounded with the mundungus of deathly men and scruffy youths; the smell of her like Dee, a memory that gets muddied by the physical presence of this Mary.

"Was?" she asks. "Is this his last book?"

"Oh, no. He's still writing. It's my dad that I meant," I say.

"Oh, God! I just didn't think. That's young."

"An accident," I say.

She smiles a sad smile and I just look at her. "So, what's it about? The book."

"It's about a load of crazy people living in a big house together in Ireland. They don't have much money so they eat onions."

"Sounds familiar. What's good about it?" she asks.

"It's funny and...bawdy," I say. She bursts out laughing.

"Bawdy? Who says 'bawdy' these days. Sorry!" She snorts. I feel hot again and my armpits prickle again.

"It says it on the back. I haven't read it myself," I admit. She hands me back the book and I put it back on the shelf.

"I thought you were going to buy it?"

"I just realized I have to buy some... some dinner," I lie.

"You can read it here, if you like?" She points to a beaten-up Chesterfield sofa over in the corner near the self-help section. Funny, I think that's what I was doing. This book will reveal deep hidden secrets to what Joe was feeling. Will it? It will, won't it?

"I've got to get back." I shrug and the contents of the plastic bag jump about in my hands as I do.

"Well, another time. I'll be here."

"You do work here then?"

"Nine to five, seven days a week," she says.

"Really?" I say.

"No," she laughs again, "I'm only messing. I'm part time, I go to college nearby, but I'll be here this week."

"Okay. Maybe. See ya!"

"See ya, Sean!"

I walk back out onto the street and toward the bus stop. I am shaking more now, and I have to let out a big fart into the noise of the street.

"Ooh!" the old granny who is still waiting says. "Excuse me!"

"Sorry!" I say.

I walk in the hostel front door and into the smell of fried meat. I tuck the plastic bag under my arm and have a quick look in the lounge, but no Jock. The Warden's door is closed and there is a muffled conversation going on in there. I don't want to get my key with this bag under my arm. Ian must be cooking but there are many loud voices coming from the kitchen, so I run up the stairs to my room anyway. I can stash the bag outside my door for a minute. When I get to it, it is open. The room is a mess. My mattress has been taken off the bed and the bed frame is against the wall, my few belongings are scattered about, my window is open and there are scuffed prints in the shingle on the flat felt roof between my room and Bumpkin's opposite. My toothbrush is out there also. "The little fucker!" I say to myself. I wash my face and get my empty holdall and put the plastic bag in it. I shoulder the holdall and leave my room the way it is and go to find Ian.

I walk into the kitchen. Tritch sees me and starts to giggle. Ian is at the stove.

"All right?" I say to the room in general. Tracksuit, next to Tritch, joins in the giggles then, which gives me a reason to stop in my approach to Ian. I try and read the room to wonder where I should put myself. I've never heard even a gasp from Tracksuit before. It could be that he is just stoned with Tritch, but there is a weird confidence to him right now. Ian is about to reply to me, but he pauses too, and I think I see him try to shush the giggling with a flick of his spatula. I wonder what has gone on here before I walked in. I take a seat. "What's cooking?" I ask Ian. I put my bag down between my legs. Ian looks at it and turns away.

"These two, by the looks of it," Ian says. "Have you just got back?" Tritch and Tracksuit giggle some more.

"Yeah," I say. "Just got some laundry to do. Have you seen that Bumpkin kid?"

"No," Ian says.

"No, why?" Tritch laughs.

"I just wanted a word with him. We have a game of pool going," I lie.

"Right!" Tritch says, laughing more. Tracksuit joins in again. I can't listen to them anymore so I get up to go and pick up my bag.

"Wait!" Ian stops me with a wave of his spatula. He moves his frying pan off the hob with his other hand and turns the heat off. A glob of meaty ragu groans and pops and rests itself in greasy redness. He walks over to me.

"Laundry room!" Ian whispers. I nod and as I leave, Ian takes off his apron. "Lads!" he says to the giggling kitchen. "Help yourselves!"

"Nice one!" Tritch says. "Eat up, lad!" he says to his new buddy.

I shoulder my bag and walk into the poolroom. There are laundry machines by the side of the tables behind sliding wooden doors. Ian opens one of those, turns on a light and we squeeze in. The machine is currently on a cycle. I place the bag on top of an industrial sized double dryer. Ian closes the door behind us both, he smells like he has worked all day, rubbing onions under his armpits for fun. Maybe he's just too close. It is hot. I am sweating, too.

"Where is it?" he asks.

"In there," I say. Ian unzips the bag and takes out the smaller plastic one. He goes to smell it and I want to tell him that it is odourless, but he kisses it instead, so I close my mouth.

"Well done, son. Well done. Jock will be chuffed with you... Right. Come on! We're going for a smoke. I want you to meet someone."

"Wait," I say, "you should know."

"What?" Ian asks.

"I think someone is looking for it," I say, and point to the package in the plastic bag that I carried about all afternoon.

"Ha!" Ian says. "What makes you think that?"

"My room," I say. "My room has been trashed." Ian breathes heavy and I want to get out of this laundry closet. He is weighing the options of his answers I guess, but I cannot get by him or the warmth.

"All right, kidder, I'll tell you what happened. But I want no trouble from you," Ian says.

"Why? What trouble?" I say.

"It was those kids."

"Bumpkin?" I ask.

"Those other kids, Tritch and them. They thought it would be funny if you went after Bumpkin. They want to see some action," Ian says. His eyes are a watery blue but they are asking me to understand something, so they are not swimming about in his head. I look away from him.

"All right," I say, "no trouble, but they'll have to put it back. The room is upside down."

"Good lad, I'll get them on it. Come on!" he says, and he opens the door and I can breathe again. He brings the bag and we walk upstairs to his room. "What did you think of Pete?" he asks me.

"He's a bit of a dick," I say.

"What else did you get up to?"

"I went to a bookshop."

"What did you get?"

"Nowt, I only had three quid." Ian stops then and digs in the pocket of his overstretched jeans. He hands me a tenner.

"Here go back tomorrow and get summat," he says as we get to his door. Tomorrow, I have been thinking about tomorrow and seeing Mary again.

"Sure," I say. "Thanks." Ian opens his door. It's a bare room, not done up with personal belongings, a few books and the same Pete is in there sitting on the chair.

"How do?" Pete says. I look at Ian quickly, but he just smiles and empties my bag and puts the package on the table.

"Hello again," I say. I am confused but I know straight away that Ian has been fucking with me. I don't let on. I play it hard. We have to be hard, don't we? Nobody likes it when we are soft. "What's going on?"

"Beats me," says Pete. "I was told to come here after I met you with the stuff."

"How did you get here? There was only one bus."

"Bike."

"He could have brought the bag for you, Ian. He got here quicker. Were you testing us?" I say. "What a waste of a day."

"Why? Did you have other plans?" Ian snaps. "Sit down, Doghouse! Sit down." I sit on the floor as Pete has the only seat. I have seen Ian snap like that at others; his mood changes quickly and the heft of him suddenly becomes menacing before he turns back into a jolly fat chef. "Not there, lad." And he points to the bed.

"Donkey called me that. My name is Sean," I say, getting up again before I sit at the foot of the bed.

"That's what he does. Nicknames people," Pete says, rolling a fag.

"What does he call you?" I ask.

"IAN," Ian says.

"MORON... He's my brother, we started that early," Pete laughs. And I realize then that I am the sucker, the idiot. These guys don't give a shit about me. I will never be a part of their family. But they don't know. They don't know that I don't want to be. I keep it all in.

"Pete, you moron! Will you cut us up some spots!" Ian laughs.

"Sure."

"Right," Ian says, "here's the thing. We were testing

you. You can't trust anyone in this place, especially not these wee burglars. Bunch of toe rags. So me and Jock thought about you, Doghouse!" He laughs.

"Bastards! And it's Sean. How did you know I wouldn't run off with your stuff?"

"Where would you go? And anyway, it wouldn't matter that much." Ian picks up the package and throws it to me. "Open it!"

Pete is busy with a chunk of brown stuff, massaging it into a strip. "What's in it?" Pete asks me.

"You don't know?" I ask Pete. He gets out some baccy and starts to roll a cigarette with one rizla paper.

"They don't tell me nothing. I was just supposed to meet someone with a package I got from a guy at the market. I thought he was a front. Then you showed up, but you seemed to know what you were doing, so I went with it. They told me to come here after. I didn't know you lived here," Pete says, licking the gum on the paper.

"I don't," I say. "I'm just staying for a bit... I am innocent!"

Ian is laughing. "Pete is just visiting. Jock wanted to see you could do it. Go on, open it!" So I do. It's well wrapped and hard to open. Pete gives me a penknife, so I cut into it, and as I get through the layers it gets softer and definitely does have a smell. Earthy. It gives me a flashback to my time with Louise and my stomach turns. These are memories that I have to put out of my mind. Places I would rather be, but I am here and I can't ever go back. There is nothing to go back to anyway. This is my life now and it is not even tethered to the old one. There are new roots.

"Mushrooms," I say before I have the package opened.

"That's right!" Ian says.

I unwrap it fully and there is a beautiful cluster of golden fungus, a little stinky and I don't know how precious. Pete is chopping the flattened brown strip he has been massaging and is cutting it into tiny cubes with a penknife. "Magic!" Pete says.

"Are you going to sell 'em?" I ask.

"God no, I'm going to cook 'em and eat 'em. I love chanterelles."

"*Mushroom* mushrooms?" I say. "You bastards."

Ian and Pete start pissing their sides laughing. I feel a little dizzy because it all feels for naught. Why did I put myself through rubbish with these criminal masterminded idiots?

"So what was all that in the laundry room? Another test?" I ask.

"I was winding you up. It was a bit intimate though, wannit?"

Pete says, "Why, what happened?"

"Nothing," I say. "Ian was trying to be funny... Bastards!" I mutter again.

They are laughing so much now that tears are flowing. It is somewhat contagious and I laugh a little at their laughing. And I feel a relief, like a seriousness has lifted and I'm not frowning anymore. I realize that my jaw is aching from it having been clenched all day. Oh. It feels good to laugh though. Ian goes to open his window, "Light 'em up, Pete!" Ian hands Pete a clear plastic biro with the ink refill removed, Pete takes it one hand and has the fag in his mouth, which he lights. The little brown spots that he has arranged sit neatly in two rows of seven. Pete sucks the cigarette until the tip is glowing, then dabs it onto one of the spots. The spot starts to smoke and Pete sucks up the thin stream of light grey wisp into the pen tube that he uses like a straw. He sucks until the dot has burnt out, then he stops and holds his breath and hands the tube to Ian. Ian takes the fag also and dabs it onto a spot and sucks up the smoke from the glowing end of the fag through the clear plastic tube until the spot has burnt out. They have a couple more goes each then Ian passes the tube to me. "There's a hole here, put your finger over it," he indicates on the tube, "and don't let too much smoke get out, these smoke detectors are checked regularly and they are a nightmare for going off."

"What is it?" I ask.

"Jesus, kid! It's just cannabis resin. Come on before the fag goes out," Pete says, but he is already rolling another one. I take the rolly off Ian, get it hot and glowing and dab a spot and suck up the smoke and keep it in my lungs for as long as possible.

"Stop!" Ian says. "Stop when the spot has gone, you'll burn your lips."

I have another go and my dizziness grows. I am stood on the edge of some massive chasm. I am a tiny speck that could get squashed between a thumb and forefinger, and yet I feel free. I feel so free to do anything. So I sit down again on the bed. Ian takes the rolly off me and douses it in the sink as it's nearly done. Time seems to slow right down. I look at Ian's books then and after what seems like five minutes of staring at one, I stretch to pick it up. It has an erotic fantasy cover, fleshy muscles and muscly flesh writhing about like a snake has just given birth to humans—*The Citadel of Undoing* by Toby Canon. "Thar's a good 'un. You can have a go of that. I've read it," Ian says.

"Thanks," I say and put it in my empty bag. "How long

have you been in here, Ian?"

"None of your business," he laughs, so does Pete. "About two months."

"Yer, his girlfriend won't let him back in his own house after what he did," Pete snickers. Ian hits Pete on the head softly, but Pete immediately looks in the mirror and primps his locks, with practiced fingers, teasing his hair gently. "Geroff!"

"What did you do?" I ask.

Ian sighs, "All right, I'll tell ya. I kidnapped the guy she was shagging and tied him up."

Pete is laughing, but I go quiet. The thought of torture chokes me. Revenge doesn't even come into my head. I had listened to Joe hit my mum when I was so young that I could do nothing. I don't even have a name for her but Mum. Mum. Mum. Ian changes topic and drones then about some other fantasy books. More spots are done and the conversation goes on and on and becomes like music in the room, tinkling and washing over me and through me into an oblivion encased in sonic cobwebs. I nod like the men in the room. Mum. Mum. Mum.

I wake up with my face in a place that is wet and sticky. It is dark around and I am prone on a carpet somewhere. I sit up and something detaches itself from my head and clanks to the floor. I can smell custard and as I lick my face, I can taste it. I must have fallen asleep in my dinner. I get to my feet and grope the wall for a light switch. There it is. I am outside a door with the number one on it. My door. I am number one. Yet I still don't have my key, and this time the door is locked. Those lads must have put it back together inside and tidied up all spick and span and done a good job and closed the door behind them on the way out this time. Maybe my window is still open, but even if I get inside the problem will remain. My key is in the Warden's office and the staff will be wondering why I have not picked it up yet. I sit down again next to the bowl of custard and I wipe my face with my T-shirt. I wonder what time it is and why. I have to get my key before the curfew when the office closes or I will be reported missing, even though I am not. I have to give an account of myself. So, I take a minute to listen—there are footfalls above, someone is awake, there are voices beneath which means that the TV is still on. I have time.

I sidle down the carpeted stair in my socks. I guess my boots are in Ian's room. The office door is open and Dan, an assistant, is on the phone. I stand in front of him. He tells the phone to hold and cradles the receiver. "What is it, Sean?"

"My key."

"Bit late, aren't you?"

"I was with Jock and Ian before, lost track of time." I say their names as a password, a word that will get me a pass and no interrogation, but it doesn't work this time.

"You were with Jock?" I realize from his tone that I have to play it cool. "When?" Dan says. "Only I haven't seen him all night and he's usually in here bending my ear."

"Dunno. I haven't got a watch... Earlier," I say. "I nodded off in the lounge."

Dan looks at me as if I am a worthless idiot and hands me my key, so I turn to go and take a breath. "Sean!" he says, and my blood pumps hard again, I know he is going to ask me about drugs, maybe he could see it in my pupils.

I turn back around.

"Yes?"

Dan makes a motion with a finger to his own cheek. "You've got something, some custard..."

"Oh! Thanks," I say and rub my face with my t-shirt again. Dan's face is a picture of disgust which makes me smile, "G'night!" I go, in fucking relief.

Outside of door number one are my bag and my boots. I open and go in, the room is back to its usual blank state. I take the boots and hang them outside my window and then I flop onto the bed. In my bag is the book, Ian gave me, *The Citadel of Undoing,* and a note that reads, "See you tomorrow, Lightweight!" I guess I am at that. I don't know if it's any better than being called Doghouse though. I turn off the light and get to the sleep that I need.

"SEAN REILLY! PHONE!" I am in the kitchen having a cup of tea. There is only one phone in the house so I make my way to the Office. Emily is on duty and she just nods at the receiver that sits on the Warden's desk. She busies herself with some paperwork and gives the impression that she is not listening. Still, I think, she is.

"Hello?"

"Hello, Sean. Is that you?" It's a female voice, a familiar voice, a voice so distant and faint that I almost don't recognize it, but I do, and I have to take a breath and bite my lip.

"Yes. It is."

"It's Dee."

"What's up?" I ask her. I keep my mouth mealy as Emily shuffles some more A4 at the desk. I turn away to face the open door and twirl the plastic cord around my hand. But it is Dee. And she's calling me. Oh my Lord. How can I not yelp a hallelujah? But I am a man in a house of men. I think of Steve McQueen. What would Lee Marvin do? Or Paul Newman for that matter? Fuck, John Wayne. This is Dee, calling me. I bite myself some more.

"How are things?" Dee says. "I heard in the Bluebell about everything. I'm sorry."

"You're home?" I say, in a deep voice.

"For a bit. It's the holidays. Have you got a cold?"

"No. Is it the holidays?"

"For us, yes."

"Right... How are you?" I ask.

"Great. How are you doing?" Before I say anything, she breathes loudly down into my ear. "I'm sorry about Joe," she says then.

I turn around and Emily is at a filing cabinet ignoring me; I have nowhere to go. The window is covered by a white, roll-down blind and the sun is beaten back but shows a broken brown stain in the very middle of it, in a horizontal line. I don't know what it means. I force myself to look at something more familiar, the Warden's certificates of service. I smile for no reason as Emily looks at me. I turn around again and want to cry. Everything seems so old and dead here.

"Yeah," I say. "It was horrible."

"So... Do you need anything?"

"Not really."

"Can you have visitors?"

"No," I say without thinking about it. "It's just blokes."

"I want to see you."

"I dunno." I have to bite my lip again. I haven't even

let myself think about her and now...

"What about coming here?"

"I can't make it there. We have a curfew. Why?"

"I can meet you somewhere in the city."

"Today?"

"Yes, today," she says. "I've got some of your stuff you left, I thought you might like it back."

"Really?" I start whispering then. "Like what?"

"Oh, some... you know... some stuff that you gave me. Can I come?"

"I guess," I say, "I'm going to..." I look at Emily then and decide to whisper, I cup the receiver "... be in the bookshop near the Cathedral. Two o'clock."

"Okay." Dee laughs, but she sounds tired, then whispers back, "I'll be wearing a pink carnation." The whispering, and my snicker, sets Emily's ears twitching, but it doesn't matter to her, or it shouldn't. I still have a tenner to get a pint or two. For all Emily knows I'm going to buy a book. I say goodbye to Dee and put the phone down. "Thanks," I say to Emily, and she grunts as she pretends not to hear me, which makes my idiot grin even broader.

I walk into the lounge. Ian is in there in the fog. "What's up?" I ask. Walnut is here too. "Tony got arrested last night. They sent him down," he says.

"Who?" I ask

"Tony! Little guy with the goatee! You know the one that nearly knocked your block off?"

"Oh him!" I can't say that I am upset. "Why?"

"Missed his curfew again!" Walnut explains. A couple of new lads watch TV static in the smoke, caught motionless for a while in their own little worlds, uncaring of what's going on anywhere else. Cathode rays are intermittently visible through the wispy breaths. The whole room reeks and makes me wonder why I spent so much time in here. "What's going on, Ian?"

Ian stares at the telly and doesn't look at me. He says something about "gossiping old women," but I can't hear him properly, so I sit on the arm of his chair and he looks up at me. "Where's Jock?" I ask.

Ian digs in his shirt pocket and hands me a piece of paper, then he puts his finger to his lips and waves me away as if he still has the creative magic of a spatula in his hand. So I take the greasy note and leave.

I go to the toilet on the second floor, just to be safe, and sit on the thing, trousers down, just to be safer, before I open the note. There are instructions, handwritten, to go with a car and get to a meeting on a farm way out of town at one o'clock, and then what to do when I get there, pay the farmer for a package. Another package! What is it with these guys and their packages? I should just become a postman! The driver of the car will have the cash we need. I guess Ian doesn't trust one of us still. Well, it's a thing, a new experience. I wonder if I'll make it back in time, but here's the other thing I think, what does it matter? And I wonder about freedom. If freedom even exists.

I do not owe anyone anything right now. Well, except my obvious debt to society, and it isn't even at that. It's just some cash I have to pay back to Woolies, or the employment agency, not to you lot, the general public. And the agency robs Woolies anyway. I guess they are up front about it though. I have an idea then that I should start paying back whatever little I can out of each government cheque that I get. That makes me laugh, but it's a thought. So what am I doing? What can I do? I can do me. I think about Mary's eyes. She was thinking of me again. I can't think about her. Back to the first thought though, can I get away with it? This time the job has to involve something serious. The last time was just a test. And where is Jock? And what has this got to do with him? Or is it just for Ian? And why has Ian become so morose and monosyllabic? Even if I do do it, am I just a scapegoat in case things go haywire? Have they already sold me out so that I get caught? Am I a decoy? And where is Jock? Has he gone? Why were the wardens so worried? And if he has gone, why is Ian getting me to do a job? Am I a decoy, a scapegoat? And should I just not do this? And should I hand it all in to the Warden in the morning? If Jock has gone, Ian is left, and I can get rid of him if I tell. As long as no one else knows, no one knows. But they always know in this place. Am I just a sitting duck on a donkey? A goat? My head. Why am I thinking? My head. I try to breathe deeply. What about Dee? And Mary? Mary will be fine, I can see her another time, but I had a feeling that she wanted something, and not just that, not just me, anyone. And what about Dee? Is she just making sure I'm okay because of Joe? Joe's okay where he is. Dee will be okay; it's been a while anyway. I'll meet this guy and do this thing. Am I decoy? A scapegoat? Do they trust me? Christ I need a beer, and to stop smoking that shit. Why me? What choice have they got? There is no peace. I rest my case and then I wipe my arse.

I can hear the gutters bubbling and I want to stay in bed. It is dark and early and dirty outside but the thoughts of this job for Ian won't let me sleep any longer. My vivid dreams are waking me, making me fit to burst. I have to get up. I get dressed and go downstairs. I make a pot of tea for everyone seeing as I'm the first up. Emily comes into the kitchen.

"Piss the bed?" she asks.

"Job interview," I say. That is all I say and walk out with a mug to watch for the car outside. I stay under the porch as the rain comes down in a sheet of water.

A blue Ford Capri pulls up and the window winds down. "Get in," he says to me. "I'm Phil!" and he flicks out his fag butt and winds the window back up.

"Reilly," I say as I get in.

"Nice one," he says. He drives us away from the street corner, from the city centre, from the immediate troubles, off and into something and somewhere else. We drive through the suburbs and by a massive green park until we are out into countryside. I wish I could walk in it again, with a dog. Why can't I just go and walk and listen to the birds? But I know why, authority, so I will ask myself no more questions. I am stuck with these guys who are all about the inside. He's older than me, Phil, and has the easy silence of a confident man. I don't speak either but it's not because I am sure of myself. I am nervous. I just can't let him know it. And we are working. Well, kind of. I let him drive and I don't ask questions. I watch the crows and I see some magpies that I count, now, out of habit, like trainee nuns, I laugh to myself.

"What?" Phil asks. I guess my chuckle was too loud.

"I was just remembering," I say.

"What?"

"Nothing. Magpies."

"One for sorrow?"

"Yeah, but there were about eight."

"I dunno what eight is for," he says. I look at him and think he was one of those kids. One of the ones I studied but could never be. He reminded me of Chizzy, Harry Walker, and Lanky, smoking, drinking, driving, and all grown up by the age of fifteen. I was wearing National Health glasses and had braces that I had to shake before I could play. "Where are you from?"

"Rochdale," I say. "How about you?"

"Wigan." There is not much more to say about it. Our towns don't belong to us. We are not even there anymore. I think about the Town Hall again and shudder at the memory of Louise again and John Bright's statue and my last good day there in Rochdale. A good bad day. But my thoughts go back to the outskirts and the canal and to our walks and to Joe and I have to shut out the memories of all that I miss. I am here now I remind myself again, again, and I concentrate on the view from the car window. We come off a single lane road to a large old stone farmhouse, it is singular in its situation. There are fields enclosed and animals bleating, clucking, and mewing about. There is a big open barn off to the bottom of a track and we pass that, with the tethered farm collie snapping at our tires as we do. Phil steers the car toward a gate through a tractor's trail and stops, engine on, sputtering in the mud. He hands me an envelope. "Go on," he says, "your turn. I can't go in there."

I don't ask him why. I'm here now, aren't I? I've learned not to ask how we got where we are. I get out, pocket the envelope in my leather jacket, and climb over the wide metal gate. I jump down, splashing wet, fresh, brown, cow-cack onto my black boots and jeans. I walk onward and before I knock, I think, this is the last time for Jock. I can't owe him anymore than this, not unless he buys me a new T-shirt or something.

"What the fuck do you want?" a voice curses from behind the old wooden door.

"Jock sent me," I say. "I have the cash."

"Oh!" the voice says.

"*Oh*, he says! *Oh!*" I mutter to myself. The door opens. A man in a suit opens the door then. He is not old. He looks posh to me. He has neat hair and is clean-shaven and has wide, hairless nostrils. His eyes are small and black but they look over every inch of me.

"Sean? Is it?" he asks. "You smell like shit."

"That's it." I am immersed in it and I can't seem to get out. "Are you Nigel?"

"Yes. Come in then. Wipe your feet." I walk in and stand in the vestibule. It feels like church, in a different way, a celebration of the history of a family. There are portraits everywhere. It's a grand house, elegant for a working farm, with foreign rugs and vases dotted about. As well as all the portraits there are antlers and animal heads bursting through the walls. There is not a thoughtless square inch of surface uncovered. I remember our house and all the trinkets we were responsible for that had no meaning. That tiny, glazed ceramic tern I bought Mum some years because it only cost a pound, she probably still has it. That kind of crap is unbreakable.

"And don't touch anything," Nigel says, "I'll be back in a mo.'"

I take my time to scrutinize the paintings. No wonder

Jock didn't want any of the burglars to come here. And I wonder on his influence with the Warden. Then I am distracted. There's a picture that takes up the whole of the wall in the main room. I edge toward it as I slip off my boots. It must be twenty feet high, portrait style. It's impressive. Obviously you can't see the eyes on eye level, but they look like Nigel's from this distance and angle. I laugh at the thought of Tritch or Bumpkin trying to lift this wonder when Nigel appears behind me.

"Grandmama!" he says.

"Yeah?" I say.

"Good isn't it?"

"It's big," I say.

"Pops had it commissioned before, well, before the crash in '86, you know?"

"No," I say. "She died in a crash?"

"Pleb!" he says. "The market." I look at him like an alien I guess. "Come on. Follow me!" I hop along after Nigel. I worry about my smelly feet as he takes me to a side room, an office, all wood and leather. "Sit," he says. So I do. I am now askance at all the similar but new visual stimuli in here that overwhelms me. "I wouldn't normally trust an oik, but listen." I look at him then, but he is not doing eye contact. He is busying himself in a drawer in his desk. He takes out a package. So, now I am concentrating. "You, whatever happens, should keep your mouth shut afterward." He looks at me and shifts the package across the tabletop. I take out what Phil had given to me and slide it toward him. Nigel opens the envelope and counts the money. "Good," he says. "I'm going to miss doing business with Jock. On your way, Sean." He doesn't look at me again, so I get up and leave. And put my wet boots back on.

Outside, Phil has turned the engine off and is dozing behind the wheel. I open the door and get in. "All cool?"

"I guess," I say. "I was told not to open it." I hand Phil the package.

"No," he says, "this is your thing. I'm just the driver now." And he shoves the package back to me.

"I can drive," I say.

"Have you got a car?"

"No."

"Well then," he snorts and we set off. I breathe a little easier at first. I close my eyes and calm my heart. Phil chews his gum and turns the radio on. I try to ignore the heavy metal and zone into thoughts of Mary, but thoughts of Dee take over. I smile in my sleepy state. I think about how our conversation will go. I wonder how to be when I see her. I ask her some questions and go through every eventuality, every possible outcome of dialogue, and she still doesn't say anything that I understand.

When I open my eyes again I see the countryside give way to the outskirts of another town that I don't recognize. "Where are we?" I ask.

"It doesn't matter. I'll get you home after. Just keep shtum, okay?" I don't say a word. I know I have to see her again. I have to keep on.

We drive past allotments and factories, petrol stations and pubs, churches, crappy looking kebab shops and chippies, deeper into town onto streets lined with red-brick houses, small-terraced ones like ours, mine. But they aren't mine, and the farther away we are the more worried I get. I feel sick, like I might puke, but I keep it in. We turn by a corner shop and park outside a house with a green door. There are some kids playing outside in the street with a dog, but it is quiet otherwise.

"Come on," Phil says, and turns the engine off. "Grab that. Time to deliver." My heart starts thumping again, but I know silence is my best option. We get out of the car and I manage to hack out some of my stomach and I pretend that it's just phlegm as I open the car door and spit into the storm drain. Phil knocks at the house as he looks back at me with disdain. There is some shuffling and coughing before the door of the house is opened by Jock.

"Come in," he says. "There y'are."

"Fuck!" I say.

"Aye!" he laughs and takes me into his arms and I smell his mundungus cardigan.

"I missed you," I say. I can't help myself; I say it like a whisper.

"I know lad, nae bother!" he says. So I just pretend like nothing happened and go inside.

We go into a small front room. The TV is on and a woman gets up, awkwardly, to greet us. She is white haired and her legs, encased in crinoline, make a synthetic scraping noise as she walks toward us. "Come in, lads! Cup of tea?"

"Aye, Hen! Get 'em a brew," Jock says. "Sit." So we all sit. Jock perches himself on half of his arse and looks at me.

"What's going on?" I ask.

Phil tuts, sucks in his breath and gets out his baccy. Jock laughs, "You know, son, you shouldn't ask so many questions."

"Why not?"

"Well, ye can. You won't get many answers though."
He coughs then and takes a puff from an inhaler. "Where
is it?" I get the package out of my pocket and hand it to
him. "Good lad," he says. He opens it up in front of us. Phil
is as interested as I am, we both watch from our
peripheries. Jock doesn't want to hide it though. He takes
out two small books, one of them is a passport. He flicks
through it and looks at the photograph, of himself, and
nods. "That's fine. That's all fine."

"How does it look?" the woman asks, as she comes
back in with mugs of tea.

"It's all good, Mary Hen!" She kisses Jock then. "I AM
OFFSKI!" Jock shouts. It's the most expressive that I have
seen him. They laugh and hug each other. Phil lights his
cigarette and looks at me and rolls his eyes. I sip my tea. It
is strong, hot, milky and sweet. It burns my lip. I bite it in
the same place that I have bitten it before. I taste blood.
We sit in silence but all I've heard today is to be quiet. I
can't keep shtum any longer.

"So what now?" I ask.

"All right," Jock says, "I'll sort you out. Mary Hen!" Jock
motions with his head toward the sideboard. Mary Hen
goes over and opens it and brings over some cash. "Pay the
lads!"

Phil sits up to attention and takes the money.

"That's not what I meant," I say, as I take the cash. Phil
sighs.

"What is it?" Jock laughs.

"What do I do next?"

"Sean. You do whatever you want. You've done me a
favour, but, more like a wee jobbie. Nobody knows you
know me, and I've paid you. We're even. I am off to

169

Marbella. I'm not dying in this Sassenach country. Just keep your mouth shut and we'll all be okay." I look at Mary Hen then, and she smiles at me. Oh. I guess none of this is any of my business, and I feel a relief not to have to do anything else. I shuffle the money in my fingers; it's two hundred quid. It doesn't seem to matter, and then I put it in my pocket and have another sip of tea. "Phil, take this wee lad back to his bed before curfew or we'll all be in the shit."

"Righto, Jock!" Phil stands up and shakes Jock's hand. "Send us a postcard." Mary Hen gives Phil a hug. She smiles at me and takes my mug. Jock rubs my head.

"Take it easy, kid," he says. "It's a long life, but yer no pussycat, you only get the one."

"Right," I say. "Have a nice holiday!"

And they all laugh at that, but I don't know why. "C'mon," Phil says as he pushes me out of the door. We walk back to the car. Phil is still laughing. "Have a nice holiday!" he chuckles.

"What?" I ask.

"Just get in and shut up."

We set off back to the hostel. It is getting dark.

Phil puts on some loud music again. He starts headbanging as he is driving, and I close my eyes for a while.

"Fuuuuuck!" is a shout that infiltrates my crazy dream and I wake up wide-eyed. We hit something on the road. I guess he couldn't avoid it. He pulls over and we both get out.

"It's only a fucking rabbit," Phil says. He turns back to look at his car. "Made a mess though!"

"What time is it?" I ask, yawning in the dark and cold.

I want someone to put me to bed.

"Shit, come on!" And we get back in the car and zoom off again.

We are late. I am in trouble. Phil drives away quick like after he drops me, and I have to knock on the locked door of the hostel.

"Sean." The warden is waiting for me.

"Sorry!" I say and I give my most attentive and apologetic eye contact.

"You've been a good lad, and a you can play a bit of footy, but I can't have this coming in late," the Warden says. He stares at me, but he can see that I am not drunk or drugged up. I hold his stare. He sighs.

"Sorry! I went for a job interview. Out of town. On a farm."

"You need a reference? Because I can tell them that you are not all that punctual!" he laughs. "Go on with you. Last chance though, mind! You've got court again tomorrow!"

"Oh, yeah," I say. He knows everything. I wonder if his leniency with me is because I'm white like him, but I keep my mouth shut. "Thanks!" He throws my key at me; I catch it and walk out and up the stairs. It is quiet in the house—the only sound is that of locking up. None of it matters. If you can get away with it.

There is a tapping on my door that rouses me from an eye rolling dream about earless dead rabbits and noseless dead dogs, floating bloated and gross down a muddy canal towards the biggest waterfall.

"Wake up, Reilly! We need you!" The voice is urgent but not loud. It sounds like Tritch. I wake fully. *"Reilly?"*

"What? What is it?" I ask the voice.

"We need you," it whispers.

"Tritch?"

"Yeah, it's me. C'mon!"

"No joke?"

"Serious, man!"

"Alright. I need a piss."

"Room five. See you there in two shakes!"

I hear the footsteps recede. Room five? That's Bumpkin's room. Something is up. I get dressed.

I knock on the door of room number five, quiet as I can. It opens. Bumpkin is sitting on his bed. He looks terrified. The room smells of sweat, it is hot with breath. There are six lads in here, standing around. Tritch and Tracksuit are the only two I know.

"What's going on?" I say.

"This cunt has been caught thievin'," Tritch says.

I look at Bumpkin again, it seems that he's been crying, his face is red with welts. I guess these guys have punishment first on their minds.

"What's he done?"

"Dave had a hundred quid under his pillow this morning," Tritch nods at the lad with the perry haircut. "He's next door. This is the only fucker who could have it."

"What's it to you?" I ask Tritch.

"Dave's a mate. And we don't steal from each other."

"Right!" one or two of the others say. That makes me laugh.

"We're all fucking thieves," I say. It's one thing I've learnt in here. "Did you take it?" I ask Bumpkin. He looks at me, sniveling, his eyes glassy and dark, he spits on the floor. He doesn't deny anything.

"Why are you asking me to do this?" I ask Tritch.

"Because you've been in here the longest," he says. And it's something that shocks me. Time has gone. People have gone. I've been in here that long. They need me to tell them what to do, how to be.

"What about Ian?"

"He boosted. I think he went with Jock." There is no one else. I get it. Jock and Ian were looking at prison time so they did a runner. I knew – the passports!

"Yeah, I figure he did," I say.

"Well," says Tritch. "What shall we do with him?"

Bumpkin won't look up at me - thief, liar. He stares at the floor. I wonder what he wants, why he's such a dick, but I don't really care.

"It's nowt to do with me," I say. But I can't see him pasted by six of them. I remember my first night here. I ask everyone to leave the room. They get angry with me. They wanted to kangaroo him regardless. And Bumpkin knows. But they asked me in to sort it out. So, I get five minutes.

"They are going to kick the shit out of you," I say to Bumpkin when we are alone. "Maybe worse." He's a sniveling wreck, but it's not weird what he did. He wanted a reaction. I know why. He needs a name, to be a part of the gang. No one likes him.

"I know."

"You want that?" I ask.

"Maybe," he says. Maybe he wants to prove he can take the punishment.

"Give them double the money back. Maybe they'll let you off."

He nods. Then shakes his head.

"They'll never let me in."

"You're a burglar. You'll find a way." Bumpkin nearly laughs at that. He sidles over to his mattress and takes out more than he stole from the other guys. He hands it to me, sheepishly, and locks his door when I leave.

Tritch has no reason to freak out after I give Dave the money. They are all impressed.

"That little greasy fucker," Tritch says.

A few of us go to his room to do some spots and talk about nothing we like. Things get loose right there as we giggle into the night. Life changes fast. We are fluid and can forget ourselves, disappear even, like the smoke we make. None of us will live here forever anyway.

I go to the bookshop in town and as I hop off the bus, Dee is there, waiting at the stop. It's a thing to see her. It's not been that long but the sight of her short shock of red hair thrills me. She doesn't see me and I suddenly feel self-conscious. I sniff myself. I can't do anything about that now, so I go over and tap her on the shoulder. "Hullo!" I say.

She turns then and grins and takes my hand in hers and shakes it. "Sean!" We look at each other. "It's good to see you," she says.

"You too," I say, and I swap hands to my left so that I am by the kerbside, and she still wants to hold it, so I hold it for longer and we bump on along the street to the shop together. I can't let go of her hand, even when it is sweaty, and it's alright, I think, it's more than us just seeing each other again. She grips me though as we walk down through the bustle of the town and stops me to look into my eyes.

"I'm pregnant," she smiles. And it happens just like that, in the blink of a uterus, after the last spasms of a drunken night a few months ago. I know what she is saying and why she is telling me. I get something in my eye then, a piece of grit or something. Not really, but I pretend so. I see a way out. I look away for a moment, one moment that she lets me have for now, then, I look back at her and think about how happy she seems. I need to know that she is happy. Her eyes make me smile. I feel, like a jolt in my balls, that there is something else in the universe, another way to be. I don't have to be this me anymore. I feel reborn in that blink. Maybe I can be someone else. Even then I know it's not all about me. Shit.

"It's good? You're good?" I ask her.

"It is," she says. "No worries." She rubs my head. "Well, lots of worries," she says, "But, not really."

"Not really?"

"No, Sean. Mum and Dad are great... I just had to tell you. We've had a lot of time and a lot of talk about it. That's why I came back. It's only right that I let you know. We've had time. I know you haven't."

"How is it? I mean what are you...What about university? What do you mean we?"

"I mean my folks. We've decided what to do. I'm going to come back here to study. And we have a plan, if you want to hear it? They want to help you, Sean."

"Oh! *That* we. We should go sit down," I say.

We go into the bookshop. I start looking at spines on the shelves, out of habit and distraction. Maybe I should look for a baby book but I spy the Donleavy I wanted and let go of Dee's hand. He might have better advice anyway. What does anyone know? "I thought we were going to sit, Sean," Dee says.

"Yeah. I'll get us a tea." She goes over to the beaten-up Chesterfield and I take my book to the till from... Oh. I'd forgotten about Mary, or did I? She is the reason I was coming here, but she isn't now.

"Hello, Sean!"

"Hello, Mary!"

"I'm glad you came back," she says. Her cat eyes are on. "What do you want?"

"Two teas, please."

"Two? Why thank you!" She puts the tea bags in the mugs and fills them with hot water. "Can you help me with something?" she asks. "In the back there."

'Sure." I follow her into the back there.

We are close now, I have my back to a bookshelf, the Philosophy section, where no one else is, just me and Mary. She grabs, not grabs, but it is a forceful movement, then cradles my dick through my jeans and whispers, *"I can't wait to hold it when it's hard."*

"Why?" I can't think of anything else to say. "What's going on?"

She sighs then. "Simon is so boring. He's always off swimming. Training. Preserving his energy. Come on," Mary says. "Don't you want to?"

"I don't know." I tremble.

176

"Don't you remember?" But don't I remember? "What it was like that one time at that party at that Mark's house in Norden … all night?" A tiny jiggle of some minor tremor sparks my memory and wantonness. I could forget myself with her again. Her hand moves up onto my belly, then she wraps her arms around me and pulls me into a kiss. I have nothing for her. She feels that. She is scaring me and I shrink away from her touch, but I have nowhere to go. "I see," she says.

"Sorry," I say. "Dee is here." Mary's eyes change and she wipes her hands on herself.

"She is?" Mary says, "Great." She pulls back from me. "Is she getting the band back together?"

"I don't think so," I say. "Maybe… She's pregnant. I think we are. I think I got her pregnant."

Mary slaps me. "You are a useless piece of shit! Why didn't you tell me?"

"Yeah." I say. "Ouch! Sorry? I should have. I was about to…" Then she backs off.

"Dee is ex machina! Oh! Oh! I have to go and talk to her. I can't believe you!" She says.

I go to the toilet as my nose is dripping slightly red and I need a tissue. She has hit me hard but I'm not about to cry about it. I'm going to *have* a baby. Well, I'm not. But I am. I don't care about the blood right now as I look in the mirror. What a day, I say it to myself. Will there ever be another?

I don't know what they are talking about, Mary and Dee, they are laughing when I come back out. It's a loud, snorting, carefree laughter that lifts into the air then trickles down the walls and drips into the bookshop and tickles all the customers. I guess Dee *is* getting the band back together, so I sit at the counter and drink some tea and leave them to it. Dee comes over after a while. "We need to talk, remember?"

"Well I have somewhere to go now," I say. "I can't stay here."

"That's alright. I can come."

"Okay. I guess. I have to go to court."

"I know. I'm with you." Dee and Mary hug as we go.

We are outside the courtroom, in the rain, waiting for my call to appear. Something comes over me and I manage to get to a wall outside and throw it all up. What did I even eat? I retch heavily a few times, my ribs hurt. It is mainly bile, I think. My eyes are ready to pop out of my head with the involuntary efforts of my solar plexus. My eyes are weeping. Snot is dribbling. It's all a bit much.

"Jesus, I didn't know you could be so dramatical," Dee says and scratches her nose. "You know you are not that attractive right now?"

"I'm sorry. I don't mean to not be." I retch again. I thank the rain.

"Look, just get this over with." Dee says, "Where is Lillicrap anyway?"

"He's still in there putting it to them." I cough.

"Just calm down. It's going to be fine. You'll have a place now with us. You will have a fixed abode. An abode! Anyway, that's all you need to get out of that place. You said so yourself."

"Yes. I just... every time I come here I expect the worst. I feel at the mercy of mercilessness."

Dee laughs and squeezes my hand. "We'll be right," she says. "When I heard about you, what happened and where you were. I just wanted to help. So did Mum and Dad."

"It's not all about me anymore though is it?"

"It never was," Dee laughs. "We'll find out what it's all about."

As we go back in to court my name is called and I am summoned to appear in front of the three ghouls again. Most of what is said is blah blah, and I still feel slightly nauseous and stunned, but I am empty. The upshot is that I have been released into the custody of Mr. O'Neill, Dee's dad, and can leave the bail hostel. Of course I still have to report to the Probation Service every week and keep my nose clean. And turn up for sentencing in three weeks. Lillicrap assures me yet again that it will just be a matter of paying the money back, a fine, a slap on the wrists. He tells me to get a job to make it look like I am an upstanding citizen. None of that seems to matter now though. They seem like small things, really small things, like tiny peanut size things swimming about, lost in a massive amount of amniotic fluid.

Dee waits for me on the step outside as I go back into the hostel one last time to get my shit together. I shudder as I shut the door on room number one. There is no one downstairs that I know, except for the Warden. He is busy with papers. I stand in the hallway and look about the place after I hand over my key. Some lads walk past me on their way to the kitchen. No one says hello, or goodbye.

"Fuck you," I say, under my breath to the walls and the stinky carpet and the *Lounge* and the *Kitchen* and the ghosts of those who have escaped the place. And then I walk out and away from there.

"Okay?" Dee asks.

"You fancy a pint?"

"No!"

"Lemonade?"

"Go on then. You know, you're going to have to tell your mum she's a granny."

"I know. She'll *love* that."

"She'll get used to it. Life is not a book, Sean! It goes on and on. We can make it how we want."

I squeeze her hand as we walk towards The Turk's Head. I am resigned.

"Once upon a time," I say.

"Shut up!"

About Atmosphere Press

Atmosphere Press is an independent, full-service publisher for excellent books in all genres and for all audiences. Learn more about what we do at atmospherepress.com.

We encourage you to check out some of Atmosphere's latest releases, which are available at Amazon.com and via order from your local bookstore:

Tree One, a novel by Fred Caron
Connie Undone, a novel by Kristine Brown
A Cage Called Freedom, a novel by Paul P.S. Berg
Shining in Infinity, a novel by Charles McIntyre
Buildings Without Murders, a novel by Dan Gutstein
Katastrophe: The Dramatic Actions of Kat Morgan, a young adult novel by Sylvia M. DeSantis
SEED: A Jack and Lake Creek Book, a novel by Chris S McGee
The Testament, a novel by S. Lee Glick
Shining in Infinity, a novel by Charles McIntyre
Mondegreen Monk, a novel by Jonathan Kumar
Last Dance, short stories by Nicole Zelniker
The Fleeing Company, a novel by Kyle McCurry
Witches & Vampires, a novel by Brianna Witte
On a Lark, a novel by Sandra Fox Murphy
Ivory Tower, a novel by Grant Matthew Jenkins
Tailgater, short stories by Graham Guest
The Quintessents, a novel by Clem Fiorentino

ABOUT THE AUTHOR

Born in 1970 in Burton-upon-Trent, Anthony C. Murphy grew up in Lancashire. He has had many jobs, a few dogs, and three children. He has worked and performed at spoken word events in the UK, and the USA. *SHIFTLESS* is his first novel. He currently lives in Yonkers, New York.

CPSIA information can be obtained
at www.ICGtesting.com
Printed in the USA
FSHW021740240220